SPACE FORCE

BOOK ONE: SHADOW SQUADRON

ALEISTER DAVIDSON

BLACK MANTIS PRESS LLC

JOIN MY MAILING LIST

Sign up for my newsletter to stay up to date on future releases and receive special offers:

https://www.aleisterdavidson.com/mailing-list/

Lieutenant Bonn's heart raced so fast he could hear it pounding in his ears. He could hear it over the blaster fire that turned the frigate's corridor into a red storm of death. There was little left of the pallet of cargo containers he'd taken cover behind, and nothing left of his squad, save himself. Seldom did Lieutenant Bonn panic. Space Force officers were conditioned against it. But Bonn knew he had an ice-cube's chance on Altari V of making it out alive.

His helmet had been lost when the fighting broke out. Cracked in half by a flying piece of shattered bulkhead after Captain Pern dropped a grenade. Bonn had always hated the thing, though it was bespoke and fit as perfectly as a brain-bucket could. In the moment he found himself missing it, but Bonn couldn't hold it against the captain that he'd gotten dusted and dropped a live grenade.

Without his helmet, the holoprojector on Bonn's forearm armor alerted him that his exosuit was about to pump him full of a cocktail of combat drugs. One

1

designed to bring mental clarity and focus, one designed to regulate heart-rate and blood-pressure, and one to eradicate any shadow of fear that remained in his mind.

Feeling the rush of the battle stimulants, and a sharper clarity of perception come over him from the smart drugs, Bonn knew it was his moment. He heard one of the insurgents reloading, popping another charge pack into their blaster. With his mind clear his training kicked in and took over. *When in doubt, always rely on your training.* That's what his CO always said. The same CO who was lying dead not five feet away.

Lieutenant Bonn threw a flashbang grenade over the palette with all the enhanced strength his exosuit could provide, followed immediately by two positron frag grenades. The corridor shook from the shockwaves of the deafening explosions. The blaster fire stopped. Bonn barely heard the screams of the dying, his ears were ringing with a disorienting intensity. He'd obviously done massive damage to the rebels, but without his helmet Bonn couldn't see through the toxic smoke filling the corridor. One of the frags had ruptured an air-waste line when it went off.

So he opened up, loosing a storm of deadly fury. The G-2 repeating blaster was one of the most lethal combat rifles in the galaxy, and Bonn saw why in that moment. It wasn't Republic standard issue, and he couldn't even recall when he'd picked it up. Sometime shortly after they met the counterassault, he assumed. Sometime after his head had been knocked with the force of a rhinox's headbutt.

When the smoke cleared, Bonn took a look at his work. The bits and pieces of half a dozen enemies of some unknown faction, all clad in shiny black armor, some human, some drakon, lay dead before him. Bonn chuckled a bit to himself, wondering what Captain Pern would have thought about him dusting so many insurgents without any help from his HUD. Then he looked down and saw Pern's headless body, laying across Tubs. The corridor was a bloody mess from end to end, and Bonn wanted to drift away on the ocean of blood. Drift into the sorrow he knew his heart should feel, but didn't yet. Maybe it was the combat drugs, maybe he'd just grown used to it. Used to death and carnage.

"Six dead without target lock. Not bad," Bonn said into his wrist mic, over the squad channel. Though he spoke only to ghosts.

Lieutenant Bonn took another rifle from one of the dead, reloaded his own with a fresh charge pack, and headed down the ship's main corridor toward the bridge. The deck lights were flickering and the noise coming from the klaxons was nothing more than garbled static. Bonn knew the ship was having serious electrical systems malfunctions. But that was the least of his worries. Admiral Yonk had given their team ten minutes to perform the mission. Then the Republic battleship *Vindicator* would reduce the frigate to ruin.

Eight minutes had passed already, and Bonn was the last remaining of the strike team. Weapons locked and loaded he sprinted down the corridor, past a gaping hole in the hull, and beyond the shattered bulkheads. Only minutes before he had watched as two draks were sucked out into the upper atmosphere through that hole when his team initially breached the ship. Before being led on a wild goose chase from bow to stern and back, and before the ship's depressurization sensors had initiated mag-shields. They were firing at him just before it happened, but the thought of the two draks burning up as they fell through the planet's stratosphere sent a shiver up Bonn's spine. The ceramic tiles the floor was composed of made the troopers' magnetic boots obsolete.

He got to the door, which had seemed much closer when he'd started his sprint down the corridor than it was in reality. The slicer was dead, so Bonn unrolled several feet of det-tape and made a square on the door. Without the time or personnel to hack it, he'd have to blow the door. Bonn stood back and keyed in a signal on his gauntlet. A perfect square melted through the plasteel. Without his helmet to filter the air he smelled magnesium oxide and hot metal. He kicked it in with the incredible augmented strength that his exosuit provided him, and saw into the bridge.

There was an insurgent there, in the same shiny black armor as the others. He had a blaster pistol in his hand and it was pointed at the head of a young woman seated on her knees before him, with her back to him. Bonn made eye contact with her for a brief moment before the man's voice carried through the door. From her uniform he could tell she was a Republic Planetary Guard lieutenant commander, probably taken hostage on the planet's surface when the insurgents had chosen to reveal themselves. Bonn had orders to retrieve intel vital to the survival of the Republic. The lieutenant commander was an unforeseen complication.

"Come and get her, Republican scum!" the man yelled

at Bonn. "See if she's still breathing if you come through that door."

Lieutenant Bonn, without hesitation, leveled his blaster rifle and put an AI aim-assisted round right between the eyes of the rebel. It was a mistake he'd regret for the rest of his life. As the man's head exploded in a super-heated splatter of plasma he squeezed his own trigger. The blast missed the young woman's head, but it tore through her throat. Her entire neck and spine was destroyed in an instant and she fell forward, as dead as her killer.

I didn't have time for her anyway, Bonn thought as he entered the bridge through the blast hole in the door. *It's probably for the best,* he told himself as he frantically searched the bridge. *She'd probably just slow down the mission,* was all he could think for comfort. If he couldn't find the holo-data the team had come for then all of his friends died for nothing. The entire team.

Bonn tried to push the thought out of his mind. Even the drugs weren't completely taking the shock off. He knew he'd have to deal with that day, with their loss, for the rest of his life. Just like he'd have to deal with the woman lying dead at his feet.

The countdown alarm sounded on his wrist gauntlet. Bonn knew it had been ten minutes, and that meant the *Vindicator* would blow the ship out of the sky. Bonn braced for impact beside the captain's command chair. Ironically he had dusted the captain himself, during the initial boarding action, before his helmet had been cracked open like a bad guelva melon. It always felt good to take out an enemy officer. Especially one of higher rank.

As Bonn reminisced about past deployments and the various majors, captains, lieutenants, and petty officers he'd killed since his days in Space Force, he failed to notice the ship didn't blow up. It was several seconds before he did.

When Bonn took the command chair and opened a comm channel to the *Vindicator* he found out why. Before he even hailed his ship he saw over the monitors that the upper atmosphere was being filled with innumerable hexagonal plates. Gold in color, and each side the length of several capital ships, they emerged from hyperspace one by one until the sky was gone. The daylight side of the planet covered in a dark shroud as the plates drew closer to one another.

The *Vindicator* and the rest of the Republic Eighth Fleet opened fire on the nearest panel with everything they had, but to no avail. Bonn's survival instincts kicked in as adrenalin took over. He glanced at the monitor to see the insurgents' ships also firing at the panels. Then the entire firepower of the in-atmosphere Republic fleet was brought to bear on a single golden hexagon, which only shimmered slightly when nuclear weapons impacted upon it. All other ordinance showed no effect at all, and it shrugged off the nukes in moments.

The various cruisers, corvettes, and frigates the rebels called a fleet, chose to put differences aside and fired everything they had at the same panel the Republic was targeting.

Nothing.

The massive hexagons then began to converge on one another. They came closer and closer to the planet, forcing the fleet back into the atmosphere, as plasmatic arcs of lightning danced between them. It was obvious to Lieutenant Bonn that they were going to come together like a shell around the planet. And he didn't want to know what happened after that. He certainly didn't want to be trapped inside it.

Bonn ran from the bridge, with all the enhanced strength of a Republic Space Marine hopped up on stimms, thrust into a life or death situation. He knew there was still a single-man fighter with a hyperdrive in the hangar bay. He heard his heart pounding in his ears again. Bonn found the hangar in less than a minute and saw that the fighter, an old VX-42 from the Great War, was not in flying condition. The mechanics had taken the hyperdrive out and were servicing it on a gurney next to the ship's life-support unit.

Bonn knew he wasn't getting off the planet in the fighter, but there was also a lightspeed capable shuttle in the hangar. And it would have to do. Lucky for him it was a Republic shuttle, and he knew exactly how to fly it. An S-76 cargo shuttle that had been converted into an armored personnel carrier.

He boarded it, flew into the cockpit, started its engines, and immediately began plotting jump coordinates out of the system. Bonn punched in the only place he could think of in that desperate moment. An outpost in an astroid belt in a forgotten system the Republic had abandoned long ago. The only reason Bonn even knew it existed was he was born there. It was probably not inhabited, and probably hadn't been for years.

The Lieutenant had never plotted a jump to hyperspace from inside a ship's hangar before, but that didn't stop him. The shuttle's scanners showed him the Republic and rebel fleets still struggling to dent a single one of the thousands of hexagons. And then reality blurred into a thin stream of consciousness as the ship rocketed out of the hangar, climbed hard, and the hyperdrive engaged.

Bonn was slingshotted out of the atmosphere just as two of the massive plates came crashing together behind him. A few milliseconds later and he would have been smashed between two golden hexagons with the combined mass of three Republic dreadnoughts. A bright flash streaked out of the atmosphere, off into the darkness of space, as he jumped from the system.

B onn arrived at the system where the outpost had once been, only to find the rock he was born on had been converted into a mining colony. There was nothing there for him, nothing but a moment for him to catch his breath. Bonn knew what he had to do. As much as he didn't want to, he had to return to the Gylian system. He had to get a record of what was happening. Something to show STARCOM to explain why he was the only survivor of the Republic Eighth Fleet. Though he hoped that he wasn't, Bonn felt in his heart that it was true.

And he began to sob a little. The guilt of not succeeding in his mission aboard the insurgent ship, of failing the last mission Admiral Yonk sent him on… It was more than Bonn could take in that moment, and he began to crack. Despite everything. Despite the training, despite the combat-drugs, despite the fact that he hated Yonk as a man, but respected him more than the Chancellor himself. Despite all those things, Bonn cracked.

As he sat in the cockpit, crying into his palm, trying his best to choke back his tears, Lieutenant Bonn became aware of another presence. Someone was in the cockpit with him, behind him. He reached for his blaster pistol, but his side-arm was lost on the insurgent ship.

"I'm unarmed," a young woman's voice came from behind him. "Don't hurt me. I hid in the shuttle when the shooting started."

Bonn swiveled in the pilot's seat to see a scared mechanic in her work overalls, still covered in grime and grease. She was trembling, but held out a holodisk in her grubby hand, offering it to him.

"I'm Royce...a mechanic. I'm not a soldier, and I don't care about politics. I just fix fighters, so the Coalition took me aboard. I never wanted to join them, but they made me. I think you might be looking for this."

"What is it?" Bonn asked as he took the holodisk. "Is it what I think it is?"

"I hope so," she said. "Please don't take us back to the Gylian system. Everything on that disk should tell your people everything they need to know about what happened."

"You know what that was?" Bonn asked, genuinely shocked. "You know what it is that can swallow up an entire planet?"

"Yes. I do," she said. A strange darkness fell over her face. Her mood became grim. She took the copilot's seat.

"Well?"

"They are the Vargon Empire. A force older than

many of the stars themselves. They come from another galaxy, and they feed on…" she trailed off.

"Yeah, I saw. They surrounded the whole planet. I don't even want to know what happened to everyone on it, let alone the Eighth Fleet," Bonn said.

"Planets are smashed to their constituent atoms, the iron in their cores…and in some cases gold, is used to construct more of those hex-plates…and their rings," she sobbed. It was apparent that she was shaken.

"Rings?" Bonn asked, confused.

"They smash the planets and use them for materials. But what the Vargon actually eat, what sustains them…are the stars themselves," she said.

Bonn was stunned. "So, they are like some sort of star vampires or something?"

"Exactly. Or, well, at least that's what the Coalition thinks," she replied.

"So, what? Do they build some sort of ring around a star and smash it like they were doing with that planet we just barely escaped?"

"No. They surround the star with a giant ring that unfurls like a snake across whatever system it falls upon. It comes in from a place much like hyperspace. A shadow dimension adjacent to ours, the Vargon home. When the ring fully surrounds the star it releases trillions of those same plates we saw on the planet," she went on.

"So they surround stars with Dyson sphere's? What then?" Bonn was intrigued and horrified.

"They activate some sort of wormhole, or Einstein-Rosen bridge. I'm not exactly sure what they do, but they suck the star into their dimension. It is just plucked away, right out of space. Right out of our existence and into theirs. Gone."

"And what do they do with them?" Bonn asked himself as much as he asked her.

"Nobody knows for sure, but there are rumors. Rumors that they eat them."

"This is the Republic's worst nightmare. We've got to get this holodisk to STARCOM. What is on it just became the single most important information in the galaxy," Bonn said. "Ever been to New Terra, Royce?"

Admiral Vallon Drex walked onto the turbo-lift to the CIC of his carrier, the *Kentucky*, a half-drunken disheveled mess. On his way up the lift he tried his best to comb his wild, salty hair with his fingers. He didn't want to have to break it to his crew that they were being deployed on a mission critical to the survival of the Republic. One from which they might not return. But it was part of the job. The part he enjoyed the least, except for knowingly sending pilots to their deaths.

As he passed through the automatic doors from the lift, Ensign Lowell was already trying to hand him a data pad. The young man began rattling off a list of different communications from STARCOM, though the admiral ignored them and dismissed Lowell with a wave of his hand.

Drex cleared his throat and got the attention of the crew. The Admiral had the respect of those who served under him in a way that most men did not. Many had been with him since the Great War against the Drakon

Confederation. Others had been on the ground with him on Mantalar, when then Captain Drex had led a daring mission against all odds to save a drak diplomat held captive by the mantids. He'd earned the title Hero of Mantalar that day by the Republic; though other races would come to call him the Scourge of Mantalar, or the butcher.

It was his fierce loyalty to his men, and to the Terran Republic, that helped Drex uncover the truth. That a splinter cell within the Republican central government had orchestrated the death of the Terran ambassador, and armed an insurgency on Mantalar. All as an excuse to rain biological extermination down upon the Mantid world, and seize its resources. It had been standard business for that faction of the Republic. Standard until Drex had exposed the truth, which nearly started a civil war. Over a hundred worlds had been *cleansed* in such a manner. A hundred alien races extinct across an uncaring galaxy. All to fill the pockets of a few corrupt fat cats.

"We are headed straight into the jaws of death, once again. Called upon to sacrifice everything for the Republic, if necessary. *Our* lives may just be a drop in the bucket if we die…if we fail. The whole Republic is counting on us to pull this one off. Frak, the whole *galaxy* is counting on us," as the admiral spoke palpable waves of grave seriousness emanated from him. Before he continued he made sure to look each of his crew in the eye. He set his jaw, and tensed his forehead before he continued, accentuating the purple scar that ran down his face, over his right eye, and down his neck to be lost under the collar of his uniform.

"I was briefed by Star Command less than an hour

ago. Dozens of Republican worlds have gone silent, all out on the galaxy's edge. Fleet Intelligence has provided little information, though what they have had to say is very discouraging. The stars themselves are disappearing. Just gone. Wiped off the galactic map. One of the worlds was found, flying off on a random trajectory after its star was plucked out of existence. I know it sounds amazing, and it is. But that doesn't make it any less true. What we are headed into is a situation the likes of which the Republic has never seen. They won't be able to keep the situation quiet back on New Terra much longer. Though there is a concerted effort to do so.

"And lastly, the draks have reached out to us, despite their isolationist post-war position. It seems they have lost some worlds as well, and are all too eager to blame us. The Drako embassy has informed Chancellor Krell that war may be imminent. But, through our network of spies, Fleet Intelligence became aware of a drak Commander who may actually know a little something about what is going on. We are departing now to meet him. Navigation, set course for the Lyran system."

All crew members turned to their stations as the admiral took his seat. When the helmsman nodded at the grizzled admiral the old man gave the order, "make the jump to hyperspace."

2

Commander Slaath was not used to being patient. The cybernetic upgrades that the Confederation had implanted in his brain and nervous system made sure that he was always combat alert, ready, and able. The drakon race wasn't quite as aggressive, nor as restless, as they had made him. But the cybernetics the Confederation outfitted its wounded soldiers with had proven themselves in the field, time and time again.

He sat in his command chair, upon the bridge of the *Infernal*, stroking the length of his chin. Remembering a time before his lower jaw had been a mechanical steel trap. Remembering what his scales had once felt like. Slaath turned to his communications officer, his red, robotic eye shining bright in the dimly lit ship. He didn't need to say anything more than simply clearing his throat.

"Sir, we have word that the Republic has dispatched a ship to meet with us. We should expect their arrival within the hour," the young reptoid said, as he sent the relevant comms links over to Commander Slaath's holoscreen.

"Did they say who it was that they were sending, Ensign?" the old lizard's voice showed the slightest bit of anticipation anxiety.

"Yes, Sir. It is the *Kentucky.*" The ensign knew that the news would not be received well.

"So. They have sent me Admiral Drex. Is this some kind of joke?" The Commander's rhetorical question went unanswered as he leapt out of his chair, lashing about with his whip-like tail. The vibro-blades at the tip shredded one of the consoles. Sparks flew about and the smell of ozone filled the bridge as a small electrical fire broke out. A bot descended from a hatch that opened in the ceiling and sprayed a thick mist on it until the fire died. Two other service bots came out of the lift to the bridge and set about repairing the console before Slaath had even finished with his fit of rage.

His crew had gotten used to his outbursts. Something wasn't quite right in his head since the battle of Mantalar. Since he'd had his jaw blown off by a Republican M-85 blaster rifle, lost an eye, and suffered severe brain trauma. Still, he was one of the best tacticians the Drakon Confederation had, and had the fierce loyalty of those under his command. Even unto death.

The destroyer was cramped, being a small warship typically used for support. The crew had gotten used to the conditions years before, but occasionally it felt a bit claustrophobic for Slaath. They could tell it was one of those moments as he left the bridge immediately.

"Let me know when they arrive," he said just before the lift doors closed.

3

C aptain Miller didn't like the uncertainty of the situation they were walking into. She knew that the draks couldn't be trusted. Nobody knew it better than her. She'd seen too many of her friends die at their hands, seen how merciless they could be; what cold-blooded killers the reptilians really were. Star Command didn't want to hear what she had to say during the mission briefing. To the point that Miller knew if she pressed on it might mean a demotion. It had been obvious that Fleet Admiral Valdana wanted nothing to do with her concerns, when he dismissed them as non-issues.

Miller had served the Republic well for centuries. She was the ace of aces. The commander of the elite Shadow Squadron. With her long list of achievements, innumerable accolades, and tactics and strategies bearing her name (all taught at the academy), Captain Miller wasn't used to her concerns being dismissed. Especially so effortlessly. After all, she had literally written the book on situations such as the one they were walking into. The uncertain.

Her confidence in Admiral Drex was absolute, though. Whatever the mission, wherever they were deployed, Drex had never let her down. He may have sent her to meet her death against overwhelming odds more than once, without so much as blinking an eye, but he'd never dismissed her strategic advice, nor ignored her concerns.

As she got to the Admiral's cabin Captain Miller took a moment to compose herself, though she knew that the ship's computer would have alerted him to her presence already. She reached for the bell, but before she could ring it the door opened.

"Come in, Captain," the Admiral's voice was welcoming. Not the usual stern tone he liked to use on the bridge. He offered her a drink. "Bourbon?"

It wasn't often that Miller got to imbibe alcohol. She simply nodded, confusion fading to excitement, as she took the glass of caramel colored liquid from him. He drank his whiskey neat, but she noticed that hers was on the rocks.

Before she could ask about it the Admiral explained, "it was in your file. You like your bourbon on the rocks." He motioned for her to sit.

The Admiral's quarters were nearly empty. A few chairs, a small table, the monitor screen, a rack of hangers all with the same uniform (the standard issue Republican jumpsuit in grey), and a few different tablets were all that he seemed to have. Except for a sculpture on the table. A sculpture that seemed to be carved from a strange green crystal. It was abstract, but obviously not of any human origin.

"Mantalar. That one came from Mantalar. I keep it as a reminder..." the Admiral trailed off, his eyes slightly glazing over. He seemed to drift away to some far-off place.

After a few too many moments went by Captain Miller cleared her throat and asked, "a reminder of what, Admiral?"

"Genocide. Extinction. What the Republic was willing to do to other races...what some other race may yet do to us," the Admiral came back from whatever past he had drifted away into. He composed himself and gave Miller a smile as he sipped a long drink from his bourbon.

Miller followed, savoring the burn of the whiskey on her throat. She sat for a moment, absorbing what he had said. She wondered if he meant anything by it, if he knew something about the mission they were embarking upon.

"Captain Miller, we are en route to meet Commander Slaath of the *Infernal*," the admiral became somber. "Do you know what my history with Slaath is?"

"I only know that you faced him in battle. That you nearly killed him, took his jaw and eye, left him with brain damage. I also know that he surrendered to you," she said all that she knew off the top of her head without consulting a history file.

"Indeed. That is all true. But I did far worse than that to him and to his people. The Great War was quite... *savage*. I'm not proud of many of the things I did, but I always did them for the Republic," the Admiral paused to sip his bourbon. "I am concerned because Slaath knows who I really am. Not the hero of Mantalar. The Butcher. But everything I did, I did it to prevent another war with Drako. To prevent the loss of billions, if not trillions, of Republican lives. As well as the lives of the drakon who would have died in that conflict. Slaath knows that what I did on Mantalar was to prevent inevitable conflict from consuming the galaxy, and that I was successful. For that, I have his respect. Or so our network of spies tells me. But he also knows what I did to make that happen. That I ordered the use of a bio-weapon that caused the extinction of the mantid race, allowing the Republic to seize the resources of Mantalar unopposed."

"He'd have done the same thing. If he were in your shoes…" Captain Miller said.

Admiral Drex cut her off with a stern look. A look that sliced right through her and burned her soul. "He was. We were in the shit together. Human and drakon, in the trenches, fighting hand to hand through the streets against an innumerable onslaught of mantid warriors. Slaath is the only being in the galaxy that knows the truth. That I executed the Drako ambassador to Mantalar…put a blaster to his head and pulled the trigger."

Miller was shocked. She nearly dropped her glass. "I'm stunned. You *prevented* a war by executing a foreign ambassador? And you did it right in front of drakon troops, that you were fighting beside?" Captain Miller could barely contain her curiosity.

"That's exactly what I'm saying. Slaath and I have a very complicated history between us, but nowhere near as complicated as everything that went down on Mantalar. If the galaxy only knew…" Drex started to drift away again.

He headed off to some battle long ago, on an alien world, in a galaxy that noticed little and cared less.

"He's got a reputation now as a real loose cannon. Why did they send him to meet with us? Of all the lizards they could have sent, why him?" the captain wondered.

"*They* didn't send him. He did. Which tells me that he's sincere. Or its some delusional attempt at revenge on me, though that is not the way of the drakon. Still, he's acted against his people's traditions on more than one occasion. A genius like him should be in charge of their entire fleet, but he's too much of a free thinker for their Fleet Command. And that is why I called you here," the admiral said. He took a long pause before continuing. "To let you know what kind of situation we are walking into."

"So, that is why Star Command only dispatched one carrier to the first meeting with the draks since they ceased diplomatic relations with us," Miller said, but before she'd even finished the captain knew she was wrong about something due to the sour look on Drex's face.

"Well, Captain…STARCOM does have a sense of humor. But they sent me because they are unaware of the truth of what went down on Mantalar. Slaath is, as you said, a loose cannon. It's hard to predict how he'll react. And I'm briefing you on all this because if the shit hits the fan I need someone who knows the lay of the land politically. I need someone who won't hesitate to pull the trigger."

"I'm your man," Miller said, breaking into a light chuckle.

"I know. You are my most trusted advisor, as well as too often the sword of my vengeance. I just don't want you to look at me any differently, knowing a little more about what happened on Mantalar. Of all the beings in this cold, heartless galaxy…you are the one who I couldn't stand to see lose respect for me," the Admiral leaned forward and kissed her on the forehead. A long, sincere kiss. Full of love and the concern of a thousand worried mothers.

"You could tell me you nuked Old Terra yourself…It wouldn't sully how I see you in the slightest. I've seen you tested in the heat of combat time and time again. And I've seen you triumph, with the heart of a champion every time. You will always be my hero. I'd follow you to hell without blinking an eye," she began to tear up, thinking of all the battles they'd been through. Of all the Space Force pilots and soldiers who hadn't made it back from those alien systems they'd fought across. Thinking of all the times they'd set the galaxy on fire.

Captain Miller set her drink down, threw her arms around her Admiral's neck, and squeezed him tight as if it were to be the last time she'd ever see him. She sobbed, overcome by a sense of desperation deeper than any she'd felt in two hundred years.

4

S laath sat impatiently on the bridge of the *Infernal*. His clawed hands gripped into the arms of his chair, tearing into the soft human-leather seat. His crew knew that he was in one of his 'places.' Even simple interactions could end violently, so every crewman on the ship was on edge.

Drakon ships typically had lower lighting than Republic ships, and the bridge of the *Infernal* was no exception. But Slaath kept it darker than most, preferring only the light given off by the various screens, monitors, control panels, workstations, and comms devices to any overhead source. His heightened vision could handle it, though it often annoyed some of his crew. Slaath liked to keep them on edge; never comfortable. The crew never complained to his face, and he felt that it made them harder. More combat ready.

"ETA on the *Kentucky*, Grix," Slaath demanded of the ensign.

"They are expected momentarily, Commander," the

young lizard replied. The words almost sticking in his throat in his nervousness.

"Good. Ensign Grix, open comms channels as soon as they arrive. I would speak with the humans…with Drex, before meeting them," Slaath demanded. "Lieutenant Vorn, prepare my landing shuttle, you and Ensign Grix will be coming with me."

"Yes Sir!" Lieutenant Vorn replied, saluting. He was all too eager to get off the *Infernal*.

Lieutenant Vorn had served in the Confederation Navy for longer than he could remember, and most of that time had been aboard the *Devastator*. The largest battleship in the fleet. While it was no longer the flag-ship of the fleet, it was still its pride and joy. Vorn had given everything he had, mind, body, and soul, to that ship and its crew. It was an insult to him to serve under one such as Commander Slaath. As far as Vorn was concerned, he deserved command of the *Infernal*. Fleet Command didn't see it that way though. And when he made his opinions known (in a heated session during a debriefing he'd rather forget ever happened), Vorn was demoted and assigned to duty aboard the *Infernal*.

So he did as he always did. His duty. Through gritted teeth and a clenched jaw. With all the resentment he could muster. Vorn knew that they would require a few men to accompany them on their trip to the *Kentucky*. After seeing firsthand, more times than he could count, how brutal the Terran Space Force could be, Vorn knew he'd need their most elite troops for the mission. Confederation Marines.

He didn't trust humans. Not a single one of their species. Not even as far as he could throw the *Infernal* in a black hole. Vorn often wondered how it came to be that Slaath had such a respect for the Terrans, especially Admiral Drex. *It must be his implants. There has got to be something wrong with his brain now*, Vorn thought as he headed to the mess hall.

Lieutenant Vorn knew he would find Major Bast in the mess hall. He was always there at the same time, each and every day. Gambling and drinking with other officers and a few NCOs. Bast was hard as nails, a veteran of a thousand conflicts. He'd seen engagements from one side of the galaxy to the other. Vorn knew he'd be eager to join them on the shuttle, and there was no one who he'd rather have working security when away on a human carrier. *Where is the rest of the fleet?* Vorn wondered. *The Kentucky came alone, which is quite unusual.*

Vorn entered the mess hall to see Bast exactly where he thought the marine would be. Playing cards with his men, half-drunk, but still sharp as a tack. Bast had thick plates protruding from his skull, and horns curving along his jawline. His face was a bright lime green, pitted and marred with scars from untold battles. It was a miracle that Bast still had both eyes.

The Major looked up from his game, casually meeting Vorn's stare. "What do you want Lieutenant? I assume you need me to do something you either can't, or rather wouldn't, do yourself," Bast cut straight to the point.

"Major," Vorn saluted Bast. "Commander Slaath has tasked me with preparing a security detail for our meeting aboard the Republic ship. We require your marines to provide that security."

Vorn was nervous. Though he was acting on the Commander's direct orders the Major outranked him. He knew Bast had little respect for him, after being dressed down by FleetCom, or at least he suspected it. With Vorn's demotion he lost his confidence, often finding the back and forth flexing of power and rank in the Drako Galactic Service to be an annoyance. Their culture demanded constant struggle, constant testing of dominance and capability, and Lieutenant Vorn had grown weary of it. Just as he'd, long before in another life, grown weary of war. Bast was an entirely different animal. He lived for war. He spent every waking moment thinking, eating, breathing, bleeding, drinking war. If it wasn't a fight then Bast didn't want anything to do with it. He knew what he was best at, and made it a point of only being where he was needed.

"That's why we're here, Lieutenant. We're already packed, ready to hit the loading ramp into the away shuttle as soon as they green light the mission. Anything else?" the gnarled old Croc asked dismissively.

"That will be all Major," Vorn said. His voice shook as the scales of his face took on a redish hue. "See you in the shuttle bay."

As Vorn walked back through the mess hall doors and out to the hallway the laughter that Bast's men had stifled through the whole conversation erupted. Though he knew Vorn was still in earshot, Bast joined his friends, letting out a rancorous cacophony of exaggerated noises. A moment later and he left the mess hall to join his away team.

"Men, something tells me there's more going on than their telling us. I want each and every one of you to walk onto that monkey ship ready for anything. I didn't like the way the Lieutenant was shaking. His tail was twitching and his scales were glistening with fear enzymes. Whatever this is, it ain't no average security detail for a diplomatic meeting. Stay sharp."

5

Admiral Drex was displeased that Slaath had reached out to him, that the lizard had wanted a personal parlay before their meeting. Drex thought it was bad form not to do things as by the book as he possibly could. Especially with everything that was on the line. It was bad enough that so many worlds on both sides had disappeared, but for hostilities to be on the edge of resuming after so many cycles of peace was unthinkable. And yet it had come to that. The galaxy was on the brink of war once again.

The Great War with the drakon had cost trillions of lives, seen entire systems annihilated, and had erupted into a galaxy consuming inferno that lasted generations. All based on a lie. The longer Drex lived the more he thought on the subject, and the more he thought on it the more he was sure that all wars were based on lies. At least in modern galactic history. Hell, probably all the way back to Old Terra. To back before mankind stepped out into the stars. Drex often fantasized about living before the invention of the hyperdrive, before humans had stepped out into the great expanse.

The admiral decided to go with his gut and take the old lizard's holonet call in his quarters. As much as he didn't like it, and as unorthodox as it was, Slaath wouldn't make a point of a private one-on-one conversation unless it was important.

Admiral Drex sat in his chair, placing his holo-projector on the table. As soon as he turned it on Slaath answered, enthusiasm radiating from him. The old lizard didn't seem uneasy at all, though the hologram only projected his head and shoulders. Drex's hands were shaking. He hadn't seen Slaath since Mantalar. And just the sight of the cyborg drak's face was nearly enough to take his scarred mind right back to that desolate planet.

"Admiral Drex, so good to see you, my old friend," Slaath said, opening with a kind gesture.

"Nice to see you too, Commander. It has been quite a while, hasn't it?" Drex asked, trying his best not to show how shaken he was. A little small talk would give him a moment to get his composure together.

"Indeed it has, Vallon. Indeed it has. So, you must be wondering what it is that I want. Why would the old lizard reach out to me only moments before our meeting?" Slaath toyed with Drex.

"That *is* the question now, isn't it?" Drex asked, sarcasm dripping from his voice like venom. "So?"

"There are traitors on both sides Admiral. Until their identities are known…no one is to be trusted. I have uncovered a conspiracy. One involving members of both the Confederation's and the Republic's leadership. They are planning another war. And we are expected to fight, and die, once again for their profits. Whatever is happening, it has something to do with the endless war that this faction wants to plunge the galaxy into," Slaath said.

The Admiral said nothing. Only nodding affirmatively, indicating that he believed the drak. He sighed deeply, leaning back in his chair. When he finally spoke it was with grim determination.

"Slaath, do you think that I trust you? After all we've been through. I assumed that you were coming here to get revenge on me. That this whole thing was a trap and you intended to set it in motion," Drex was brutally honest. "I did mutilate you, murder your squad, execute your ambassador to Mantalar, and…"

"Yes. Yes. Yes. You did all that. And more. I know," Slaath interrupted. "This is bigger than personal qualms. I know you did what you did out of duty. I know you acted honorably, for your Republic. I would have done the same. Including releasing the bio-weapon on Mantalar. It was not apparent who's side any of them were on, I wouldn't have taken the chance on it either. And like you, I suspect, I'd live with the weight of what I'd done crushing me under it for the rest of my days," Slaath said, as sympathetically as possible for a six-foot-tall cyborg lizard-man.

"Well…I had no idea that you felt that way," Drex lied. "I can see you are sincere. The ship's computer displays that you aren't lying. Not about any of it. I see that you at least believe what you say. And whether what you claim to know about the disappearing stars is true or not, we will find out together.

"I had a strong feeling something wasn't right

anymore with our leadership. Yours as well. STARCOM has been beyond incompetent lately. Now I can see that it has been for a reason. Commander Slaath, we must approach this situation with extreme caution. One wrong move, we could end up starting the war we're trying to prevent," Drex concluded. He pressed his fingers together, a nervous habit, and stared intently at the hologram of Slaath before him.

"You are a man of honor, and courage Admiral Drex. My only regret in knowing you has been that we have served on opposite sides, and been enemies rather than allies. We will depart for the *Kentucky* within fifteen Terran minutes," Slaath said, honesty pouring from him like a fountain. He'd always respected Drex, and there was no reason to lie about it, or even not to show it. "And Admiral, before we arrive I need you to do me one favor. I need you to pull all the files you can find in the Republic's database on a race called the Vargon. That is what we are dealing with, out on the galaxy's edge."

Then Slaath closed the holonet session. Drex was alone once again in his quarters, as he so often was. He poured himself a glass of bourbon and downed it in one large gulp, pouring another before even noticing the burn. As he sat the bottle down he noticed his hand was shaking again. He'd just heard the one word he'd never wanted to ever hear again. Vargon.

R ed lights engulfed Drex's cabin, the alert going out over the klaxons let him know that unidentified vessels had entered the system. After Slaath had buttered him up so much, he should have known it was a trap. Drex hailed the bridge as he donned his red beret. He loved putting the thing on. It made engaging enemy forces somehow feel more official. And he loved the look it gave him, and the way the crew responded to it.

Admiral Drex was fond of anything that harkened back to Old Terra, especially military garb. He was often grateful that STARCOM felt as he did himself; that it was important to keep as many of the traditions of Old Terran culture alive as was possible. Without history, without tradition, without respect for those who came before, the human race was going to forget where it came from. Many officers saw the beret as a ceremonial piece of annoyance, an unnecessary nod to the pre-colonial past of the human species. Drex saw it as a reminder of how far humans had come, and a symbol of the primacy of the Republic.

"Ensign Lowell, what's the situation?" Drex said into his wrist mic as he exited his quarters, heading toward the lift to the CIC.

"Admiral, there are four bogies approaching from behind the moon of Lyra Three. They appear to be drak vessels, but they do not respond to any known hailing frequencies used by the Confederation. If I had to guess, I'd say they are either pirates, or a black-ops team," Lowell stated. He was obviously nervous. Drex knew the Ensign had seen little action, and he hoped that it wouldn't be Lowell's first real engagement. He wasn't in the mood for that.

"Ensign, what is the ETA on Slaath's shuttle?" Drex asked, a bit of annoyance in his voice.

"He's en route now, Sir. But he's still several minutes out. Should I put you through to his ship? I have an open channel."

"No Ensign, that won't be necessary. Send Captain Miller and Lieutenant Tova to escort him. I want to make sure that he is on board, and safe. A pair of Republic F-138's should deter our new friends from trying anything funny," Drex said as he reached the lift.

6

Captain Miller had been an ace for longer than she could remember. She drilled every day, logging more flight time than any pilot in the Republic Space Force, and constantly studied tactics, operations, and past engagements. Flying was her life. It was a point of pride that she was seen as the best. Only the best of the best got to join Shadow Squadron, and after all was said and done, she was its commander.

The F-138 Spartan was her ship of choice. A single man fighter-mech capable of providing a number of battlefield rolls. It was the most dominant fighter in the galaxy, could convert into a forty-foot-tall mechanized weapons platform, and was capable of operating independently of its pilot. Space Force pilots wore an exosuit of mechanized battle armor, similar to the mobile infantry's, but lighter. It integrated with the F-138 through a series of neural uplinks, making the pilots and the ships one and the same. Syn Miller often felt naked without her exosuit, and she was glad to be back in the cockpit, though it had only been a day since she'd flown.

"Valkyrie, you are ok for takeoff," the flight crewman said. She could see Lieutenant Tova taxiing behind her.

Miller's ship shot through the tube through the main flight deck, and out into space. She knew that without the inertial dampeners she would be a mere paste inside her exosuit. As the thought crossed her mind she pushed her accelerator to the floor, and took off in a flash. Her scanners had already identified the drak shuttle and her nav computer plotted course as she picked up Lieutenant Tova. The two rocketed away from the *Kentucky* as fast as the F-138's' sub-light ion engines could carry them.

"Captain, bogies inbound. Intercept course for the drakon destroyer. Should we engage?" Tova asked, eager to see some action.

"Negative Lieutenant. Our orders are to make sure Slaath gets to the *Kentucky* in one piece. I'm sure a destroyer like the *Infernal* can take care of itself."

The two fighters took position, each between the drakon shuttle and the unidentified vessels. A red light began to blink on Miller's HUD. "Lieutenant, missiles incoming," she said, casually. Tova acknowledged by breaking off, toward the position of the approaching missiles.

"Captain, radiation scans show the warheads are nuclear. I'm going to take them out, then engage. Get Slaath to the *Kentucky*. I've got this," Tova said, confidence in her tone.

"Affirmative, Lieutenant. I'll get the old lizard aboard,

then we'll take the fight to whoever it is out there shooting at us."

Tova broke off and pushed her sub-light engines as hard as the ion drive would allow. The enemy missiles were still half a minute from the shuttle's position. She kicked off her thrusters and readied a missile pod. The nukes were closing fast as she launched her own volley of anti-missile rockets. All were direct hits, and left nothing but a quick flash and a cloud of vapor behind. Tova then took aim at the lead vessel, a frigate, and unloaded the rest of her rockets at it. Dozens of explosions could be seen across its hull as it struggled, and failed, to shoot her fire down.

"Captain, incoming fire neutralized. I have engaged the enemy, targeting lead frigate…" Tova broke off, her jaw going slack for a moment as a drakon battleship dropped out of hyperspace less than a hundred kilometers from her position.

The massive ship was oriented toward the *Infernal*. Immediately it started bombarding the destroyer with its battery of battle cannons. Plasma bursts filled the destroyer with holes as Tova was momentarily blinded by the brightness of hundreds of muzzles flashing.

"Lieutenant, return to base. That's an order!" Miller screamed over the squadron channel.

The Captain was just getting the drak shuttle through the magnetic field and into the air lock when the battle-ship arrived, but had turned right around and headed for Tova. She had to make sure that her Lieutenant got home safe, and things were about to get real hairy. Miller could feel it.

As the battleship and the destroyer pounded away at one another the frigates and corvettes that had been firing on them moved to attack positions against the *Kentucky*. All but one. Which had set course for the *Infernal*.

"Lieutenant, they've cut you off from the *Kentucky*. I'll meet you at the lead frigate, we'll take the bridge out, just like back at the battle of Cryth," Miller said. Tova knew exactly what she meant.

Both F-138's bolted at the lead frigate, dodging a hail of plasma blasts, laser fire, energy weapons, rockets, missiles, and slug projectiles as they did. Whoever the enemy was, they were relentless. Miller pushed her sub-light engines to the limits of their capabilities. She punched the controls to convert her fighter into a mechanized war-bot just as she cut the engines. Tova followed, and in a couple of seconds two forty-foot mechs were hurtling toward the frigate.

Miller slammed into the outer hull with enough force to smash a massive crater into it. She wasted no time and unfolded a colossal virbro-blade from her mech's arm. The neural interface made the motions of the giant robot's movements as natural as her own. Miller's augmented bioengineered body and mind one with the Republic killing machine. Just the way she liked it.

As Tova hit the frigate beside her, Miller was already cleaving a hole through the hull. It was only a matter of moments before they were both through. Their computer systems had given them the optimum spot to breach, but they had to deal with a series of hulls nonetheless.

"I'm going to blow the inner hull with our charge packs," Miller said as she produced an explosive pack from a compartment on the torso of her mech. "Give me your charges."

Tova handed over her charge pack to Miller and piloted her Mech out to the main hull again, turned on magnetization to her mech's feet, stuck to the ship, and waited. Miller popped out moments later, following suit.

"Fire in the hole!" she screamed, just before the fusion charge packs tore through the main hull. The ship decompressed, blowing everything on several decks out into space. Then Miller and Tova entered the breach, confident there would be no resistance as many dozens of soldiers drifted out into the vacuum, to cold lonely deaths.

But their confidence was short lived as scores of heavily armored infantry in mag-boots greeted them with a torrent of fire. Miller's mech stumbled for a moment as a rocket from a shoulder mounted launcher smashed into its shoulder. As she regained her balance she saw Tova was unloading plasma bursts and rockets into them, and they were dying in droves.

"Valkyrie, return to base, now! That is an order!" Admiral Drex's voice came over the fleet channel.

"Yes, Sir!" Miller replied. Disappointed that she wouldn't get to finish smashing the frigate and all its crew into pieces.

Tova provided covering fire from her mech's blaster rifle as Miller converted back to fighter mode and blasted off, back through the breach. She was halfway back to the *Kentucky*, dodging blaster fire from the other enemy frigates and corvettes, when she noticed that Tova never made it out.

"Lieutenant! Do you copy? Hellcat!" Miller tried desperately to reach her wingman.

She scanned for Tova and found the lieutenant's vital signs were not looking good. A moment later Tova's voice broke over the squadron comms, quiet and weak.

"It was a pleasure serving with you, sir," Tova barely coughed out the words. A bright flash tore through the battle zone, as Tova activated her suicide device, and the frigate erupted into an inferno.

7

C aptain Miller watched as her wingman was reduced to atoms. The entire frigate went nova, taking another frigate and a corvette with it. A moment later the drak battleship let loose a volley of nuclear warheads at the *Infernal*. The destroyer launched its anti-missile defense shield. A series of spheres that surrounded the ship, all armed with laser weapons capable of firing three-sixty in every plane. As the missiles approached the spheres wove a tapestry of lasers. Red blasts dissolved incoming warheads in a magnificent display of precision.

But one got through, then another. The missiles were armed with their own means of countering the missile defense. They had mounted slug throwers on each warhead, firing rapid bursts of high calibre depleted uranium rounds. The first waves may have been stopped but by the time the second wave hit the missile defense was smashed, and the nukes were threatening the energy shields.

Miller banked hard and used her targeting computer

to find the weakest point on the battleship's bridge. She got as close as she could, drawing fire from a corvette across the bow of the battleship, and unloaded every rocket, rail gun, and plasma cannon she had at the bridge of what her ship's AI was telling her was the *Black Talon*. It was an old vessel, having served the Confederation Navy since before the Great War. Still, Miller didn't pack enough firepower to even dent the energy shields. The *Black Talon* was made to take a beating, and to dish out much more.

Miller broke off her attack, taking evasive maneuvers to avoid the mass of deck mounted cannons, blasters, missile pods, and other weapons the battleship employed against single-man attack fighters. She banked away, up and over the command tower of the *Talon*, barrel rolling, and drew the fire of the corvette harassing her into the battleship. And for a brief moment, as she spun her ship around at speeds that would have smashed her to pieces were it not for the inertial dampening system, she caught a glimpse of the *Infernal*.

The destroyer exploded, solid one moment, a miniature nova the next. For a moment it appeared as if the system had a second sun. Miller was happy to put the *Black Talon* between herself and the debris that used to be the *Infernal*. Captain Miller realized that with one frigate and one destroyer taken out, what had been meant to be a tense diplomatic meeting had turned into a devastating engagement. The destroyer had a crew of at least a thousand, and the frigate probably the same. And Tova. Miller had to push any thoughts of the lieutenant aside if she hoped to make it back to the *Kentucky* alive.

Then she heard the voice of Admiral Drex in her ear, coming in over the fleet channel. "Captain, the *Kentucky* is being targeted by the enemy battleship. We have to jump, we cannot take sustained fire from a ship of her capabilities. We could launch every fighter we have, but without the rest of the fleet the *Kentucky* would still be a sitting duck, and we'd have no pilots left. I'm sending you the co-ordinates to the rendezvous point, in the Thurian system."

A notification popped up on Miller's HUD, telling her that the navigational system was aware of their rendezvous point. Then the *Kentucky* engaged its hyper-drive, crushing space-time around it as the fabric of reality disintegrated, and disappeared into hyperspace.

Miller was glad to see the *Kentucky* make it off the battlefield in one piece. She was about to engage her own ship's hyperdrive when she was notified that there was a distress signal. Someone had managed to make it to an escape pod and jettisoned before their ship was blown to bits. If she had to guess, Miller would have put her money on it being a pod from the frigate. Nothing could have gotten away from the blast when the *Infernal* went. It was one of the most spectacular explosions that the captain had seen in all her long years of service to the Republic.

Miller opened up a hyperspace comms channel to the *Kentucky*. Though she would be unable to receive a reply Miller could get a message to them by sending a burst transmission through hyperspace. It was easy enough to get a message to someone traveling faster than lightspeed. As long as they were still in the shadow dimension, and not back in our own reality, then they would be able to get the message. And Miller knew it was no short jump to the

Thurian system. It would take the *Kentucky* several hours to reach the destination. And with that knowledge Miller was able to talk herself into pursuing the escape pod through the system, and to the only inhabited body. The moon that the draks had launched their ambush from.

The drak fleet jumped, leaving her alone in the system, amongst the aftermath of the battle. All alone except for the escape pod. Just how Captain Miller wanted it. It stood to reason that whoever made it to the pod was insignificant, as the fleet had left them behind. Still, Miller liked to be thorough. Anything she could learn about the motivations of the attackers would be helpful.

She opened her voice recording channel, set it to upload to her hyperspace transmitter, and informed the *Kentucky* of her intentions. "*Kentucky*, this is Captain Miller. The drak fleet bugged out. I'm following up on a loose end. An escape pod made it off one of the frigates and is en route to the Lyran moon. I'm in pursuit. I want to see what kind of intel I can get from the survivor. I will rendezvous at Thuria as soon as I wrap this one up."

Miller scanned the pod to make sure that the survivor was still alive. She got a strong vital signal from one being, and a weak one from another. Thermal scanning showed that there had been a third party aboard but they had expired. And then the ship's AI informed Captain Miller of something that made her blood boil. The weak vital signs were not those of a drak, but of a human.

That affirmed it. The pod was from the frigate, not the *Infernal*. There had been no humans aboard the destroyer. Miller had a very bad feeling about the situation. Confederation Fleet Command had sent the *Black Talon* to silence

Slaath and his crew, which was one thing. But the fact that they were accompanied by at least one human was another revelation altogether.

"Lionel," Miller said to her ship, who she'd jokingly named after an ex-boyfriend. "Can you scan the human on board the escape pod and tell me if they are tagged with Republic ID?"

"Of course, Captain," the ship answered in a relaxing voice. Miller had found that even in the heat of battle she preferred her ship to speak to her as calmly as possible. Other pilots were different, some preferring intense, angry, or overly dramatic. Some needed that sense of urgency to remind them they were in a fight for their lives, or even the lives of others. Miller didn't need that. Just a calm, steady voice to keep her relaxed. An added element of stress was something that she didn't want anything to do with.

"Scanning complete, Captain. Yes. The human in the pod is none other than Lieutenant Commander Blick, of STARCOM," Lionel said.

"Thank you, Lionel. Now I know I did the right thing by sticking around to check that pod out. I just hope that the *Kentucky* is still in the Thurian system when we wrap this one up."

The moon of Lyra was inhabited by dozens of species. It was a trading port for merchants, though it was out on the galaxy's edge. Its remote location, just outside of Republic space, had made it into a den of pirates. There were more humans than anyone else, though Lyra had never been under Republic control. It was neutral in the Great War, and remained so. As far as the Lyrans were concerned they would always be neutral. The moon was dominated by several large cities, sprawling metropolises that contained the majority of the citizenry. The rest was desert. Miller hated the desert. She'd rather spend a decade on a frozen rock ice world than a day in the desert. And that is exactly where the escape pod landed. Smack in the middle of a vast ocean of sand.

According to her scanners both inhabitants of the pod survived the landing. Miller was entering the moon's upper atmosphere, soaring in at thirty thousand kilometers an hour, a white hot rocket cutting through the sky. She was thankful that it was night on the side of the planet the pod landed. It would make the sandy environment more tolerable. As she approached the pod's position Miller scanned for weapons, finding only a blaster pistol to be aboard. The drak probably had it. She had nothing to worry about. Even if she had to get out of her mech her exosuit would be able to sustain blasts from the pistol with a ninety two percent certainty that she would sustain no injury, and less than a one percent chance she'd be fatally wounded.

"Lionel, let me out next to the pod. I see that they are still in the immediate vicinity," Miller ordered her ship. "Then I want you to fly a loop, ten kilometer perimeter should do. I want to know if anything is coming."

Lionel fired the retro thrusters, descending vertically into a perfect three-point landing. Miller slid out of the cockpit, down a chute, and onto her feet on the ground. The bottom hatch closed and Lionel ascended, then flew off to follow his orders.

Miller approached the pod, whose main hatch was

popped open. The body of a dead drak was laying on the ground next to the hatch. Two bots were standing over it, ostensibly examining the body. One was shaking its head, the other issued a series of beeps in response as it had no head to nod. The taller one was a dull grey medical bot, ubiquitous on Republic worlds and elsewhere throughout the galaxy, though as far as Miller knew the draks had never used them. The other bot was half the height of the medi-bot, a cyber-mech slicer bot that hovered on repulsors. They were a rare sight anywhere in the galaxy, one of the most expensive bots on the market, though they were *never* on the market. Miller had looked into buying one when she'd been promoted to Captain and received command of Shadow Squadron. There was a three cycle waiting list, and they cost over two hundred thousand credits for the bottom of the line. And this unit was the upgraded package.

"Hey, you bots! Where are the drak and the human? Where's Lieutenant Commander Blick? In the name of the Republic, tell me," Miller said, leveling her M-85 blaster rifle at the medi-bot as she approached.

"Don't shoot," the robot replied in a whiney voice, holding up its hands. "We're with the Republic!"

The little slicer bot beeped a few times and a series of lights lit up across its dome.

"I don't care who you are. Where is Blick?" Miller fired a round from her rifle, next to the medi-bot's head.

"He's still inside the pod. Along with Corporal Fenn of the Confederation," the bot replied. "I am XJ-13, Republic medical cy-bot. I have made sure the Lieutenant Commander is as comfortable as possible, but he needs to be treated at a proper medical facility. It is then your duty, as a Republic officer…"

"Don't tell me about *my* duty, bot," Miller said as she stepped over the body and brushed past them. "Blick is a traitor to the Republic. Possibly the human race. He needs to be questioned, and be brought to justice for colluding with a hostile enemy force and taking up arms against the Republic. He'll be executed for treason, bot. So don't frakkin' tell me what my duty is, or I will scrap you in a heartbeat. You hear me?"

"Yes, Sir," XJ-13 replied. "I do hear you. But there is much you do not yet know."

"Then help me get him off this rock and to a Republic hospital. That is *your* duty. Besides, I outrank him. If anyone is giving orders around here to Republic bots, it's me," Miller said. She hated arguing with robots, which she found herself doing all too often.

Miller poked her helmeted head into the pod and saw the drakon Corporal Fenn sitting cross legged just inside, and Blick laying on a makeshift cot created out of the cushions of the escape pod's seats, emergency blankets, and extreme weather gear.

"All right drak, hand over the weapon. I know you have a pistol. Comply, and I'll make sure you get off this rock alive. Resist, and I'll end you right here," Miller said. It wasn't the first time she'd used that same introduction, or one very similar, but she felt a little rusty and questioned if her delivery had been taken seriously. The HUD in her helmet informed her that it had, as the drakon was breathing more heavily.

"No need for violence, human. You may have my

weapon," Fenn said. "It will not matter in the end. We are *all* dead already, and we don't even know it."

"What do you mean, drak?" Miller asked as she took the blaster pistol, handle first from the Corporal.

"The Vargon come for us all. Their empire shall reign. Their shadow falls across our galaxy, and we shall be their feast," Fenn said, a crazed look coming over him as his eyes glazed over. Miller was no longer sure whether Fenn was talking to her, or to some invisible person. He seemed to be looking through her, and around her, but not at her.

"Well, that doesn't sound very pleasant," Miller said. Choosing to acknowledge what Fenn was saying rather than to ridicule him for it. "But right now, my concern is the man in this pod. Lieutenant Commander Blick. I need to get him out of here. He needs a doctor."

"Mon Tarley. The spaceport. It is the closest city to us. I have been there many times to trade. Before I joined the Confederation Marines," the drak replied, seemingly coming back from whatever far-off place he drifted away to. "But the Republic isn't exactly welcome there. They don't like your kind, out here, on the edge of the galaxy, on the fringe."

"They like credits, don't they?" Miller asked, rhetorically. "Lionel, I need you to proceed to a local spaceport called Mon Tarley. Give me a basic recon report and find me a hospital," Miller said aloud, though there was no reason to.

Republic Space Force pilots had a live vid-feed. The *Kentucky* was out of range for it, but Lionel saw and heard everything she did, and had already located the hospital through accessing local maps over the holo-net. "Already on it, Captain," the ship replied. "Transmitting co-ordi-nates to your HUD now, Sir."

"Well done, Lionel. In that case get us to Mon Tarley, ASAP," Miller said, cracking a smile. Sometimes her ship's efficiency still surprised her.

"ETA to your position, thirty seconds," the ship replied.

8

The *Kentucky* received Captain Miller's message before Admiral Drex had a chance to meet with Commander Slaath, who was kept waiting. The drak Commander thought that he'd been entirely forgotten about during the commotion of the fight, choosing to remain on his shuttle in a lonely hangar bay, on a lonely deck, of the largest fighter carrier that the Terran Republic had ever constructed. Slaath could get out to stretch his legs and walk a mile before coming upon another soul. He began to wonder if he'd made the right choice.

Obviously he'd hit a nerve. Otherwise the Confederation wouldn't have sent the first fleet to destroy the *Infernal*. Somebody on the inside had become aware that he knew there was *somebody on the inside*, working against both the Confederation and the Republic. Slaath had his suspicions, but it no longer mattered. If the first fleet had been deployed against him then he had been labeled an enemy of the state. As such he would be a wanted criminal. And under Confederation law, he'd be executed without a trial. The Confederation would have no inclination to hear what he had to say. And then it would be too late.

And so Slaath found himself an enemy of his people for trying to save them. For at least trying to figure out what was happening to all their worlds on the edge of the galaxy. Aboard the human ship, and with his own now destroyed, Slaath began to feel desperate and alone. His crew usually would have been trembling in fear in such a moment, but Slaath was unusually calm. And when he realized the truth as to why, he consulted Major Bast.

Slaath sat with Bast alone, in his quarters, talking only between the two of them. The other officers and marines were trying to make sense of their situation in the common area, cramped as it was with all of them in it.

"Major Bast, I think that I may have grown bored. We sit here, as this ship hurtles through hyperspace, waiting for Vallon Drex to show his face. I tire of this. I would walk to the CIC and speak with him myself. You will accompany me," Slaath said, matter-of-factly. As if it were the only, and obvious, choice.

"I do not think that wise Commander, but this day has been unorthodox indeed!" the Major broke out into laughter. "Shall we take the marines?"

"No, Major. You will do. Your reputation alone should strike fear into the hearts of every monkey-man on this ship. I'm sure they've all heard of your...*deeds*, Major," Slaath said. Half to reassure himself, half to remind the Major just what a badass he actually was.

The Commander and the Major exited the shuttle together, to find themselves in a cargo bay. It seemed to be a place where no one ventured. A forgotten bay, on some lonely deck, of a ship the size of a city. Slaath knew that if he could find a comms station then someone would put him through to an officer who might be willing to rectify the situation. After walking through the massive hangar for a quarter mile they found a transport. It was an open topped buggy on four wheels that ran on a hydrogen fuel cell. The humans typically called them Jeeps, though Slaath had often wondered why. Once he'd even researched it at the Confederation Library on Virilia Prime only to find that the humans had no idea what the word meant, only that it came from Old Terra. They knew that it had been the name of a military vehicle in the age before Terra expanded into the galaxy. But whatever bigger meaning the word once held, if any, the humans had forgotten millennia before.

"Major, let us ride to the lift and get ourselves out of this forgotten emptiness. You drive," Slaath said.

Then the Commander lifted his wrist to speak into his mic, to let the ship know what the plan was. He was not shocked to see that comms weren't working. There had been a lot of action as they were boarding the *Kentucky*. Perhaps they'd been caught in the EMP after a nuclear blast, but more likely Drex had closed their channels or disabled their devices. Slaath knew going into the situation that meeting Drex would be much more complicated than meeting any other officer in the entire Republic Space Force. They would have a ton of personal history to overcome before basic diplomacy could start. So, with the survival of both races, of the very galaxy itself at stake, Slaath decided to let it all go. To forgive and forget everything Drex had ever done, to the drakon as a people, to him personally, and most especially to the extinct mantid race.

If only he could convince Admiral Vallon Drex that he was sincere. Then he knew that the first hurdle to saving the galaxy would have been overcome. But dealing with the monkey-men was never as easy as it should be. Something about how their brains were wired made them deceitful. It wasn't their fault, really. It was simply part of their nature, he'd concluded many years before.

They drove the Jeep for another few minutes, driving past many fighters, mechs, fighter-mechs, shuttles, artillery pieces, landing vehicles, escape pods, and tanks in various states of repair and disarray. Slaath recognized one of the tanks as a model that hadn't been fielded by the Republic since the Great War. They had indeed been forgotten in the dust bin. As far as Slaath was concerned, it was a massive insult. But it was one he'd have to swallow if he hoped to even begin seeing eye to eye with Vallon Drex.

Slaath knew that under any other circumstances he would have attacked with all his marines. Fighting to the last man and dying on the *Kentucky*. As it was, the galaxy needed saving, and only he held the means to do so. Slaath had told no one about the holo-cube he'd acquired, at great personal cost. A piece of technology from the lost civilization of Mantalar. And on it was all that was known by that dead race about the Vargon. Or at least all that remained of their knowledge.

When they got to the far end of the gigantic hangar, they found the door to the lift open. Slaath and Bast entered, caution thrown to the wind. They had no time to worry about anything hairy going down. If the humans took them out, then they took them out. Slaath at least would be able to die with the knowledge that the humans would be in possession of his holo-cube. And if they had his cube, there was still a chance that *somebody* could learn enough about the Vargon to defeat them. It was a one in a million shot, but it was the only shot he'd have if the humans acted without honor.

Slaath noticed the control panel had few buttons on it, but one was clearly marked Bridge. He knew that it would get him to the main deck, so he pressed the button. In a moment the two reptilian officers were ascending the lift tube. It seemed to need to be lubricated, as the lift pod ground against the tube at every seam. Floor after floor went by, each as tall as the hangar bay they'd been in. Slaath got a feel for how colossal the *Kentucky* actually was. It would have been able to dock several of his own lost vessel on any one of the dozens of decks. And indeed, during the Great War, the *Kentucky* had carried entire fleets of destroyers into battle. It was once the flagship of the Republic fleet, and had wrought ruin upon the very heart of the Confederation. The *Kentucky* had deployed the squadron that leveled the capital city on Drako Prime. The very homeworld of his people.

After several minutes of traveling through the lift they stopped and the doors opened. The lift opened into a hallway, busy with officers and crew scurrying about in their endeavors. Written on the wall opposite the lift doors were the words Bridge, with an arrow to the right, and Engineering, with an arrow pointing left. Slaath stepped off the lift, and out into the hallway, followed closely by

Major Bast. The two drew quite a reaction from the crew, and several marines arrived within seconds, weapons drawn.

"I am Commander Slaath of the Drakon Confederation. I demand to see Admiral Drex immediately. It is a matter of galactic importance and time is of the essence," the Commander said. "Your security forces should have been aware of our arrival, as we were escorted into a cargo bay by two Republic F-138s."

"Stand down men!" the sergeant of the squad who'd arrived on scene ordered his men. "This is our guest, commander Slaath."

"Thank you, Sergeant," Slaath said as cordially as possible, though he was nervous. Major Bast merely grunted in derision.

"I have been instructed to escort you to Admiral Drex's quarters. I apologize for how the crew reacted. We have been at DEFCON 2 since the attack. I'm sure someone must have assumed you were invaders," Sergeant Tran said, trying to hide his embarrassment. Most of the galaxy found racism tasteless, but the Drako were a known exception. Still, Tran knew he was representing the entire human race when speaking to Slaath, and didn't want to portray humans as barbaric. He knew that the crew's reaction had been one of fear.

"It is quite understandable, Sergeant," Slaath replied.

They walked down the hall for a few dozen meters and arrived at Drex's quarters. "I'll leave you here, Commander Slaath. Go right on in. You and the Major are expected," the sergeant said. "Oh, and I just wanted to say sorry again. About the crew...I doubt any of them have actually ever even seen one of your people before. Not in the flesh."

"Sergeant, really. It's okay. You are just overcompensating at this point. I fully understand. If humans suddenly appeared aboard my vessel, then I would expect a similar reaction from my own crew," Slaath lied. He knew his crew would have attacked first, and asked questions only if there were survivors. Still, best to let the human feel like the barbaric one.

"Of course, Commander," the sergeant said, so nervous he saluted Slaath before walking back toward the lift.

Slaath reached out to ring the bell when the door opened on its own and he heard a deep, gravely voice he'd not heard in many years. A voice full of hardness, and regret, that commanded attention. The voice of his most hated foe, and his most respected adversary.

"Welcome aboard the *Kentucky*, Commander," Drex said. "Major." Drex nodded at Bast, then motioned, at a chair.

The Major took the offered seat as Slaath and Drex shook hands in what was a very awkward and telling moment. Drex did not let go, and looked Slaath square in his one good eye.

"It means a lot to me that you reached out before your shuttle arrived. I have silenced all communications from STARCOM, and all outgoing comms as well. Sorry if that affected your systems," Drex took the initiative in the conversation, still holding tight and shaking Slaath's hand. "And I must also apologize for leaving you out in that cargo bay for so long. Something came up, and it couldn't wait. But because of it I was able to verify, with absolute certainty, your claim of traitors on both sides."

Drex let go of Slaath's clawed hand as the Commander's eye widened. "I am glad that I do not need to try to convince you, Vallon. I was worried that we would be starting this meeting on shaky ground."

"Well, there is still the matter of the attack. In the back of my mind, I have to admit, it all feels like a set-up. But I'm willing to take the chance. Billions of souls have already been lost. Our common problem is much more important, so I am gambling on the hope that you and I see things the same way. The fact that you came here at all tells me I should trust you."

"We are on the same page, Admiral," Slaath confirmed. "This piece of art on your table…"

"Yes. It's from Mantalar. After what I did…One way I deal with it is to collect art from their culture. Sometimes I sit here and look at it, and the ghosts of the past speak to me," Drex opened up. Bast could tell that Drex had few he could truly confide in, just as Slaath did. The major noted to himself that the commander and the admiral had already become best friends, though neither of them was yet aware of it.

"While it *is* art, it is also something much more," Slaath said as he produced his holo-cube from a pouch on his belt. He placed the cube within a hollow square area of the sculpture and it began to slowly hum. An undulating sound pulsed as the sculpture began to glow with an inner light. Then a beam shot up from the top of it, and projected a fuzzy hologram.

"By the tail of Zork," Major Bast exclaimed, invoking the name of the first great leader of their race.

The hologram was unlike anything that they had ever seen before. It seemed smokey at first, then began to coalesce into the form of a head and torso. In moments it looked solid, and real. Unlike any hologram used by the Confederation, or the Republic. The being in the image was neither human, nor drakon. It was an altari. A race that had gone extinct before the first human had seen the light of day. Archaeologists and anthropologists throughout the galaxy, of many different races and origins, studied their culture. They were widely believed to have been the first intelligent culture the Milky Way produced.

The altari was humanoid, with an elongated skull topped with a crest that looked much like a sail. It had light blue skin, six fingers on each hand, and pale yellow eyes that looked kind and warm. A calm radiated from the being, even as a hologram, and they could all tell that it was a very intelligent, and empathic creature.

It began to speak after taking a low bow. "Greetings. I am Korith, of Altara. I make this record of events in order for future citizens of the galaxy to understand the dire situation we found ourselves in. The galaxy has been assailed by a race of unimaginable power. A civilization from another reality, with an unquenchable thirst for the stars themselves. They are known to us as the Vargon Empire, and they have devoured system after system. Every world inhabited by the altari is now gone, their suns eaten. From what we can tell they deploy massive rings around the stars they wish to consume. They arrive instantly, coming through a pocket dimension very similar to hyperspace. The rings then activate a massive wormhole, sucking the star away into their pocket dimension, where it is stripped down and consumed.

"These star-vampires, as we initially understood them, have destroyed our civilization. Everything our race toiled to create, for thousands of generations, gone in an instant. A thousand stars, snatched from the heavens, taken away to a dark shadow plane and devoured. I make this chronicle only to inform future intelligent races who may find it, as there is no hope left for our people.

"Though it will do us no good, perhaps some future person will benefit from our tragedy. And from our successes. The accompanying star map reveals the location of a moon where we altari provided sanctuary for a Vargon defector. It is the being from which we learned all that we know of their race, and their sinister agenda. Their race is immortal, and no passing of time will have an effect upon them. Provided the Vargon Empire does not find it, the defector can most likely be found on the moon."

The room was silent as the hologram faded and a star chart was projected from the sculpture. A distant system in the mid-galactic core with a small M class star and six planets shone red, marking the spot. Though it was far from their co-ordinates the system was in a quadrant familiar to both Drex and Slaath. And less than two lightyears from Mantalar.

"Not a short journey, even through hyperspace. It

could take a week or more," Drex said. "And I'm still waiting on Captain Miller to return. She'll be bringing a STARCOM officer. A lieutenant commander who was aboard one of the drakon ships that attacked us. And hopefully one of yours as well, Commander. A Corporal Fenn, of the frigate *Corintha*."

"Captain Miller...I'd like to commend her myself. Yes, we must wait for her. She showed incredible restraint in getting my shuttle to the *Kentucky* when the shit hit the fan," Slaath chuckled to himself for using the human colloquialism correctly. "She took the time to complete her mission, making sure I was securely aboard, and then took the fight right to them. A true warrior. She is to be admired, Admiral."

"I know, Commander. She's my daughter."

9

Captain Miller had a predicament on her hands. She had two captives, and two bots, and her ship only had room for herself and one more. Their only chance was to make it to Mon Tarley and hire a crew to take them to the fleet. The bots were too valuable to leave behind. They contained critical information on the current situation. Anything they had observed would be retrievable from their databanks. The dying Lieutenant Commander Blick was her most pressing concern, though Miller admitted to herself that she didn't know what to do about the drak. Her gut instinct was to interrogate, then dust him.

She went outside the pod and consulted with XJ-13. He was a medi-bot, so he had a good AI to bounce her thoughts off. Miller already knew what Lionel would say to her. Kill the drak, take Blick to the *Kentucky*, and leave the bots behind. They could always be retrieved later. That's what Lionel would tell her to do. But in her gut, Miller knew that it wasn't the answer. Sure, it was completely by the Space Force operations manual. Technically everything in that plan was a correct action. But Miller wanted to get all the intel she could. And that included from the bots, and from the drak.

"XJ, give me some advice," Miller said. "What should I do about getting Blick to Mon Tarley, along with you two bots, and the drak?"

"Well, Captain, I would suggest taking Lt. Commander Blick to the hospital in Mon Tarley aboard Lionel," the bot answered immediately. It had been thinking the situation over, Miller could tell. "Leave Corporal Fenn's blaster pistol with me, and I will watch over him. From Mon Tarley you will need to requisition a ship to take us all back to the *Kentucky*."

"Okay, bot," Miller said, handing over the drak's blaster to XJ-13. "I'll call you on Shadow Squadron's closed channel. I'm patching you in now."

Miller keyed in a few button presses on the datapad housed in the left forearm of her armor. "What's your little buddy's name?" Miller asked, pointing at the hovering slicer bot.

"Oh, him. He's KV-1N. Most humans simply call him Kevin," XJ said. "And he's not my *buddy*. In fact, if truth be told, I cannot stand him. He is a bit of what you humans refer to as a *smart ass*."

A series of beeps issued from the slicer bot. Miller couldn't understand it, she didn't speak cy-bot, but she could tell it was pissed. A hatch on its front opened up and an arm extended with a cutting wheel whirling. Kevin didn't approach XJ, but he did threaten the larger bot with the tool.

"Look, I really don't care what problems you two have with each other. The fate of the entire frakkin' *galaxy* hangs on my mission. *Our* mission. You got it?" Captain Syn Miller had not conscripted a bot in many years, and it felt odd for her to do so.

"Got it!" XJ-13 said, lifting the blaster pistol to show he was ready. Kevin let out a series of beeps that Miller disregarded.

Corporal Fenn helped Miller to load the wounded Blick into Lionel's cargo space. There was just enough room for a space marine in heavy power armor. If someone genetically modified, a giant among humans, and wearing the heaviest, most resilient armor in the galaxy could be evacuated from a battlefield in it, a single wounded desk jockey in dress fatigues certainly could.

Still, it took quite a bit of effort for them to wrestle the dying man into the space. As soon as Blick was aboard Lionel, XJ-13 pointed the blaster pistol right at Fenn's chest and motioned for him to have a seat on the sand. Captain Miller rose vertically to an altitude of one hundred meters and then blasted off to Mon Tarley.

The journey was quick, only about a ten minute flight. She could have arrived in seconds, but Captain Miller didn't want to fly faster than a conventional aircraft. She didn't want to alert anyone that a Space Force pilot was on the lyran moon. Things would go much more smoothly if she could get in, get Blick treatment, hire a pilot, and get out. Anyone she had to tangle with would just slow the mission down, and could possibly get herself or one of her companions killed. The last thing she wanted, and the last thing the galaxy needed.

When she got to Mon Tarley she was a bit taken aback by just how small it actually was. There were a few blocks in every direction, emanating from a downtown square that seemed to have a permanent bazaar, but that was it. Otherwise there was a spaceport just outside the town, less than a mile away. While there were cities on the moon, Miller could tell that Mon Tarley was not one of them. It was more of a glorified watering hole than anything.

"Lionel, I see a good place to set down, just beyond the eastern edge of the town," Miller said as she used the fighter-mech's computer to analyze the buildings and determine which was the hospital.

When she found it she detached her neural interface, and exited the ship. Miller wasn't going to take any chances, so took her blaster pistol and a slug thrower for back-up. It was only a half-mile walk to the hospital, across the town. According to scans ninety percent of the population was at one of two locations. A cantina, and a brothel. One next to the other. It seemed there wasn't much to do in Mon Tarley. She switched to infrared on her helmet's imaging systems and saw that there was at least partial staff at the hospital.

Her walk across town was uneventful, and she drew no attention, though she had been ready for anything. Too much hinged on her making it back, and making it with all four who had escaped the drakon frigate. If she failed, the galaxy faced annihilation. She kept reminding herself of that.

When Miller got to the hospital a dull red neon light flickered on the outside of the building. The standard red cross that let anyone from one of ten thousand worlds know that they could enter and receive medical treatment. She pressed the buzzer and a robotic eye on a folding arm came out of a hole in the wall.

"State your business," the robot's vocal amplifiers rattled. "Are you injured?"

"No, but…"

"Then you have come to the wrong place," the bot responded, retreating back into the wall it extended from. The hatch it came out of closed loudly, with a *thunk* sound as it sealed.

Miller rang the buzzer again. This time when the bot answered she was ready.

"State your…"

"Captain Syn Miller of the Terran Republic Space Force. I demand entry immediately, or I will reduce this building to ash and ruin," she said, fury in her voice. "Chop chop."

The robot retreated back into the wall, and then the door opened, depressurizing the building. Miller stepped inside and into a reception room. There was a waiting area and an android nurse behind a counter.

"What can I help you with Captain?" the nurse asked with a smile. Miller had always hated the fake politeness of androids in service jobs.

"I have a wounded officer aboard my ship, across town. I need to get him here immediately, to have him examined, and treated as best he can be in a facility such as this," Miller spat at the android.

Within seconds three nurses and two doctors had entered the waiting area through a door beside the nurse's station. "Where is he? Take us to him," the lead doctor said.

"Do you have a ride? I don't really want my fighter to be seen, and if I can keep it outside of town I would prefer it."

"Of course," said the doctor. "Nurse Klink, have my ambulance meet us outside."

The android pushed a few buttons on a control panel, the front door opened, and Miller found herself loading into an old Rhinox class armored personnel carrier from the Great War that had been converted into an ambulance.

The drive took less than a minute. When they got there everything seemed normal. Lionel was still parked where she'd left him. No sign of other lifeforms. Miller got the help of two of the medical crew and they put Blick into the ambulance.

"Get him back safe, take care of him, try to patch him up. I don't know what's wrong with him, but I need this man alive. Am I understood?" Miller asked as she held the doctor she spoke with by the arm.

"Affirmative, Captain," the doctor returned, wrenching himself free from her iron grasp.

"And if he comes to before I get back, you are not to speak to him. Nobody is. He is a traitor to the Republic, and will be executed. But before that I must learn what he knows. It is vital to the survival of every single being in the frakkin' galaxy. Not to put *too much* pressure on you doc," Miller laughed. It was all she could do.

"I understand," the doctor said as he loaded up.

10

Miller walked to the cantina. She was determined to get a drink. Hopefully she would be able to find a pilot who could take them all off the rock they were stuck on. It was like most other dives across the galactic outback. Out on the fringe there wasn't much, but every town had its watering hole.

The air was smokey, thick with odd alien smells. Various strange creatures sat in dark corners consuming all manner of food and drink. Miller walked up to the bar, finding an empty stool, she sat down between a crixian trader and a man who was speaking with a lyran. The man wore the pants of a Republic officer, faded and used looking, and a navy blue leather jacket. The lyran wore only a bandolier over his hairy torso and was armed with a repeating blaster across his back, and a hand cannon holstered on his right thigh. Miller could tell they were pirates by the look of them, and pirates were exactly who she was looking for.

The bartender, a seven-foot green-skinned trolgoth

from the Vinnari system, gave her a nod as she placed her helmet on the counter. "I'll have a whiskey, the best you got," she said.

"You look like a Republican," the bartender said as he poured her drink into a filthy glass. "We don't see too many of ya'll out here on the fringe," he said as he pushed the glass toward her with his finger, never breaking eye contact with her. He licked his forked yellow tongue across his thick lips in anticipation of her answer.

"Yeah. I'm a Republican. The best goddamn pilot in the entire fleet," Miller said. Then she threw back the entire glass of whiskey as if it were a shot, wiped her mouth, then gave her glass a tap.

The bartender filled it up again. "You mind me askin' what you're doing out here? Out on the fringe?"

"Yes. I do."

"Well, aren't you something? Just walk in here, out of the blue, knock back some whiskey, and you got nothing to say?" the bartender laughed. "You're the most interesting thing that's happened in this town in quite a while, darlin'."

"Don't call me that. Who's got a ship? I need a pilot who can take three of us off this rock," Miller didn't bother mentioning the bots. She figured that she'd bring them up if and when she got to talk to a pilot.

The bartender simply nodded toward the man next to her, pointing at the lyran as he cleaned a glass with a dirty rag. Miller cleared her throat, trying to get the man's attention. Nothing. She brushed against him slightly. Again nothing. She leaned around the man, looked the lyran square in the eye, and said, "I'm trying to hire you guys. You oblivious, or just don't talk to Republicans?"

The lyran tapped his friend on the shoulder, who sighed deeply, turned around and greeted Miller with a handsome face, and a gleaming rakish smile. "Captain Felo Krynn, at your service," he pointed at his chest with his thumb. "This is my first-mate, Mister Brilliax. But you can call him *Lemmy* ," he pointed at the heavily armed, scraggly looking boar-man. "We all do, that's just what he goes by. Always has. Now, what can we do for you?" He winked at her, nearly triggering her gag reflex.

It wasn't everyday a human met a lyran. They were a rare species indeed, even on the moon of Lyra. Still, Miller was incensed. She knew the man had heard every word of her conversation with the bartender, yet he acted oblivious. And his acting was hammy, overdone, and ridiculous. It was apparent that he was hitting on her. She didn't have time for some conceited smuggler's childish games. "I need a ship. I need to get myself, a wounded prisoner, another prisoner, and possibly two bots off this damn rock and back to my fleet. You get us there no questions asked, and the Republic will make it well worth your while."

"Well, that's sorta the thing…" Krynn stroked his clean shaven chin. "We aren't exactly…how should I put it?"

"You're outlaws. Fine. I really don't give two fraks. Not only will we pay you, but I will personally make sure that whatever charges you are facing disappear," Miller said, desperate to get moving.

"One million credits," Krynn dropped his smile, a

roguish gleam in his blue-grey eyes caught Miller's attention. She knew he was deadly serious.

"Done," she said, extending her hand. He took it and they shook. "But we leave immediately."

"You're the boss, Captain…?" he reminded her she hadn't introduced herself.

"Miller. Captain Syn Miller, commander of Shadow Squadron. And if the fate of the entire galaxy didn't rest on my getting back to the *Kentucky* I'd be collecting the bounty I assume you have on your head myself *Captain* Krynn," she said with deadly seriousness. "As it is, outlaw or not, you get to step up and be a hero. Because if I fail in my mission, there may not be a galaxy left for you to spend your million credits in."

"Aye-aye, Captain," he said, mockingly, as he saluted her. "We're in the only spaceport in town, bay forty-two. We leave whenever you're ready."

"I'll get my prisoner from the hospital, then I'll meet you at the hangar bay," Miller replied. "What is your ship called?"

"She's the *Banshee's Lament*," he said. "The fastest ship in the entire fringe."

"Yeah, I've heard of it. I'm the one who blasted your scanning dish off when you ran the blockade at Ventillus IV," Miller said, as Krynn's jaw dropped. "Make no mistake, Krynn. I don't trust you. I don't like you. If I didn't absolutely need you, I'd put a blaster round right between your eyes, collect the bounty you have on your head, and laugh about it. But you have my word, as an officer of the Republic Space Force, that I will honor our bargain."

"Good enough for me, Syn," he said, turning to leave the bar with his first-mate Lemmy.

Krynn was approaching the door, heading on to the hangar to prepare *The Lament* for passengers, while Miller slammed back another whiskey, payed the bartender from her account with a flick of the wrist, and donned her helmet. All as a very large gorthian came in the door, looking around savagely, his gaze taking in the whole room before finding what he was looking for; Captain Krynn, who was right in front of him. Though that was no surprise to Miller when she saw that the thing had one large eye that dominated its head. The gorthian's chest was heaving, he was breathing so hard, and in two of his four hands he held swords...if they could be called that. Heavy, brutal, cleavers that were rusty with old caked blood. It wore nothing but a loin cloth, of some shaggy animal fur, and sandals that appeared to be fashioned from someone's skin. Otherwise the beastman had only spiked bracers on his wrists, and a menacing smile on his face. His blue-grey skin was observably sweaty, even in the dim lighting of the cantina.

Miller turned to see Felo Krynn and Lemmy approach the monster, Krynn with his hands held up non-threateningly. "Zorlock, buddy, how've you been?" the pirate asked, his voice dripping with insincerity.

The gorthian laughed, a deep, throaty laugh. One of his empty hands touched a small device belted about his waist, hidden by the fur of his loin cloth. Nothing seemed to happen, and then a piercing screech split the air. A high-pitched wailing noise, that was obnoxious, but Miller failed to see how it was effective. Then she noticed Lemmy drop to his knees, then curl up on the ground, desperately pawing at his ears. Trying to get the noise to stop. Miller understood. The gorthian knew its quarry. But to Miller it was just another rhinoxshit game that she didn't have time for.

"Gorthian! What is his bounty? I will pay it, and them some. Directly to you. Just let Captain Krynn go. He's needed on official Republic business," she plead with the bounty hunter, trying to speak as peacefully and authoritatively as possible.

Zorlock snatched Krynn up with his empty hands, one about Krynn's throat, and the other about his right arm. The giant alien held Krynn a foot off the ground. He showed no signs of having heard Captain Miller. She knew that he would not reply to her. More rhinoxshit she didn't have time for.

Before the gorthian could tear Captain Krynn limb from limb the distinctive *click-clack* of a pump-action slug-thrower cut through the commotion. All eyes in the cantina went to the green trolgoth bartender. "Take it outside Zorlock. You know the rules. And if you don't turn that damn high-frequency transmitter off I may just plug you anyway. Now, get the frak out," he said.

"I cannot believe you'd take this pirate's side. You know what he did to me…" Zorlock said, still clutching Krynn. Lemmy still flailed about on the floor in agony, though nobody else in the cantina seemed to notice anymore.

"Take it outside, Zorlock. I ain't takin' anybody's side. Except for the side of my cantina. You know this is bad for business," the bartender lied. It was the best thing that had happened in his bar in several cycles.

Zorlock complied. He drug Krynn out the door and into the street. He even had the courtesy to drag the pirate a couple doors down, so he wasn't in front of the cantina. Several patrons followed them outside. Lemmy was just starting to get to his feet, and dust himself off, but Miller was already out the door. She wasn't going to let anything happen to Krynn. She needed him too much.

Zorlock threw Krynn to the ground and the Captain hit hard, kicking up a cloud of dust. It took the air out of Krynn, and he just laid in the dirt waiting for the blades to shred him to pieces. The gorthian was standing over him, rubbing his lower hands together in anticipation, and scraping the two swords together, which sent a shower of sparks over Krynn.

The giant alien lifted both swords in a flash, they glistened for a moment in the streetlights. Then he swung them both down in deadly arcs, throwing the entirety of his weight and strength into the blows. But they never connected. Krynn had anticipated mutilation, but was simply clobbered by the body of the gorthian falling on top of him. The thing was double his weight, and it was difficult for Krynn to get out from beneath the alien, but he was alright, and it was dead.

When Krynn got out from beneath it he noticed that its head had exploded. Miller stood behind it, about ten meters away. She had used a pop-up, wrist-mounted rocket hidden in her armor to take Zorlock's head off. She had only one shot before the thing swung its blades and tore into Krynn, and she knew that her blaster would probably not kill it. Gorthians were strange pachyderms, with hides thicker than a gallbull. They felt no pain, and could grow back lost limbs. She didn't want to take any chances. Not with Krynn's life.

"Looks like you owe me one, *Captain*," she said through her external mic, making her sound somewhat robotic. She turned to face the crowd who had assembled behind them.

"Step back! Nothing to see here folks. Official Republic business," Miller said, acutely aware that she was not on a Republic world. Just some far flung moon on the galaxy's edge. An outpost that the fringe pirates and smugglers called a trading post.

Miller wondered what kind of government they actually had out there. She laughed to herself when she realized the trolgoth bartender with a shotgun was most likely it.

The small crowd, comprised of over a dozen different alien races from the far corners of the galaxy, dispersed. Most went back to the cantina. Lemmy came out, his head throbbing, still walking a little off from the disorienting effects of the gorthian's device. He laughed at Krynn as the pirate dusted himself off.

"Wachoo, mobani noga!" the lyran chided the captain.

"Screw you, Lem," Krynn retaliated. They both had a good laugh.

"Ok, now that I've saved your sorry excuse for a skin, can we get back to business?" Captain Miller asked them, after they were done joking around.

"Yeah. Thanks, Captain. You really saved my ass back

there," Krynn said. "We'll see you at the hangar bay asap."

The two pirates headed for their ship as Captain Miller went on to the hospital, her patience exhausted, and with one less trick up her sleeve. She hoped the bots fared better with the drakon prisoner, Corporal Fenn, than she did at finding a pilot to take them off the moon of Lyra. But with her luck, she figured they'd have either skinned Fenn alive and gotten nothing out of it, or he destroyed them both and got away. Either way, she didn't really care. Syn Miller was tired, and she just wanted off that damn rock a parsec from the middle of nowhere.

11

D rex, Slaath, and Bast now knew what it was they were dealing with. Basically it came down to a phase three civilization, on the Kardashev scale, using the Milky Way galaxy for food. A race as old as creation, who'd evolved over billions of years. A race of star-vampires that would see both the human and drakon races as nothing more important than insects, possibly less important than bacteria. The sentient races of the galaxy were both at their mercy, and completely insignificant to them.

"These Vargon…they are the real enemy, of both our races," Drex said, plainly. They could tell by his tone alone that he was forlorn that the galaxy was on the brink of war when it should be uniting.

"Indeed, Admiral. Indeed," Major Bast said. "Our only hope of survival is to work together. And even then…"

Before Major Bast could finish his sentence the klaxons rang throughout the deck, "arriving at the

Thurian system in two minutes. Arriving at the Thurian system in two minutes." There would be another alert when they were about to exit hyperspace. It was tradition, though exiting the strange dimension that allowed faster-than-light travel was no longer as jarring an experience as it once had been. It had taken centuries for humanity to get it down just right, but when they did they had the universe at the tips of their fingers. A mere button's press away.

"The rest of the Fifth Fleet awaits us when we arrive. I'm reluctant to contact anyone outside of my direct command, with the situation being what it is. Major Bast, I'll restore comms. Let your men know that we've prepared much more adequate quarters for them than the shuttle they are cramped into, or some forgotten hangar bay," Drex said. "Commander Slaath, would you accompany me to the CIC?"

Slaath was shocked. No drakon had ever been invited onto the bridge of a Republic ship, especially its most sensitive stations. Not once in the long history of relations between the Confederation and the Republic had it happened. "Of course, Admiral," Slaath said, bowing deeply. "I am most honored, my friend."

And with that one word, Admiral Vallon Drex knew that Commander Slaath, his once hated foe, would take a blaster round for him. That the lizardman even used the term friend was of immeasurable significance. In the Drako culture it was not taken lightly. And whether their friendship was predicated on the desperation of facing extinction together, or on respect, did not matter to Drex. Only that they were friends.

"The honor is mine, Commander," Drex said, though he was drowned out by the klaxons outside his quarters.

"Now emerging from hyperspace. We have arrived at the Thurian system."

A few seconds passed and then red alert lights came on, the klaxons blaring the distinct siren that let Drex and his crew know that the ship had been boarded. The sirens were interrupted by the computer announcing,"Blaster fire detected on decks two, three, six, seven, and nine. All fire teams, proceed to engage. We are at DEFCON One."

Drex turned to Slaath, urgency apparent on his hard face. "Can you get your marines into the fight? We could use the help, I'm sure. Because whoever is assaulting us is already aboard, and they didn't breach. Which means their tech is out of our league."

"Major Bast, send your men to the designated areas. Engage only enemy forces. Admiral Drex, I will need you to patch my men into your troops' systems, and let them know we are coming into the fight. I don't want any of my men killed, or injured, by friendly fire. If my gut is serving me correctly, then this boarding party is comprised of both humans and draks," Slaath said. His concerns were warranted.

Major Bast got on his wrist mic and contacted their shuttle, deep in the bowels of the *Kentucky*. He reached Lieutenant Vorn, briefed him on the situation, and the Confederate Marines disembarked from their landing shuttle. Lieutenant Vorn and Ensign Grix stayed in the shuttle, with two marines to guard both them and the lander.

The rest of the marines flew down the deck of the hangar bay, arriving at a pair of six-wheeled vehicles that would get them to the lift, and hopefully into the action, quicker.

S ergeant Snett felt the rumble of explosions going off throughout the ship. On the way up the lift the marines could smell ozone. Snett tasted the air with his forked tongue. There were electrical fires on the deck they were headed to, which was obvious before the lift doors even opened.

"Keep an eye out for Space Force Marines, and Republic soldiers. We aren't in this fight alone. They know we're coming, so let's get in there and give these monkeymen some relief! Oorah!" the Sergeant exclaimed, getting his men ready to kick some ass.

Then the lift doors opened.

It was a scene of absolute carnage. Red human blood splattered down the corridor of deck four. Bodies every-where, or rather, parts of bodies. It seemed as if a Dorinian cyclone had picked up a barrel of red paint and spun it down the corridor. Snett went out of the lift first, scanning left and right in the infrared spectrum. His helmet's infrared sensors let him know that the most recent footsteps had gone left. Toward the engine room.

Snett ran as fast as his power armor enhanced legs could carry him. Through the bloody footprints, toward the engine room, and over dozens of dead humans. Some were marines, like himself, twisted and contorted in death. They'd been hit with some sort of energy weapon who's effects Snett was not familiar with. Others were pilots in their exosuits. The elite of the elite. Space Force's pilots, in their mechanized fighters, were the most badass warriors in the known galaxy. Even Snett, a die-hard Croc, had to admit that. As much as he'd like to be the best of the best himself, he knew the Spartans held that title. To see so many of them dead in the corridor made his heart plunge into his stomach.

"You see that, Sarge?" one of his men asked. It was a rhetorical question, but Snett shook his head yes.

Snett stopped in his tracks, twenty feet from the engine room door. Though there was nothing on his HUD when scanning for lifeforms he heard movement in the engine room.

"They're in there. My bet, sabotaging the engines. We have to stop them," Snett said over the squad channel. The marines all concurred, nodding in agreement. "Greck, give 'em the ole one two," he said, telling his corporal to toss in a flash grenade followed up with a fragger.

"What are we facing, Sir? It won't show up on scanners..." Greck said, nervousness showing as his hands shook. He stole himself, then proceeded to ready the two grenades.

"We'll see Greck. Get ahold of those nerves," Sergeant Snett said. "On my mark. Three...two...one...go!"

Greck leaned around the open blast door to the engine room, threw the two grenades, and yelled, "frag out!" He hesitated for a mere fraction of a second before the first one detonated. Just long enough to see what appeared to be a drak, in black power armor, materialize out of thin air. And just long enough to catch a blaster round in the face.

Sergeant Snett, though standing only a few feet down the hallway, was watching over the squad holonet and saw Greck's head pop from from the marine's own point of view. It made Snett lurch forward in anger, and almost throw up his last meal.

Whoom! went the flashbang. *Kra-thoom!* went the frag grenade.

"Go! Go! Go!" Snett yelled as his squad poured into the room.

The flashbang didn't seem to do much, but the frag grenade tore through several soldiers, human and drak alike. All dressed in dark black armor. All kitted out with some sort of cloaking device that made them invisible to scanners, and it appeared the naked eye. Snett realized this as one who was not killed, but would soon die, seemed to blink in and out of existence.

Snett kicked him, realizing he wasn't going anywhere, he was just invisible. The squad unloaded on the wounded. There were no standing orders to take prisoners. It was kill or be killed, Snett knew from experience. Especially when dealing with an obvious black ops force, fitted with extremely high tech kit.

Snett sent the feed of their action over to Major Bast, who didn't answer. By the sounds echoing through the ship the fighting was still raging fierce on more than one deck. He wondered if Slaath and Bast were engaged in a firefight.

"Make sure they're all dead, then sweep the engine room for sabotage. I doubt they had time to plant explosives, with how fresh their footprints were when we hit the deck. But it's possible," Snett ordered.

Klaxons silenced the red alert signal momentarily to announce,"Bandits inbound! All Spartans to their fighters! All crews to the flight decks!"

The klaxons went back to blaring the red alert signal. A moment later a pilot's voice came through across all open channels. Bast must have patched them in fully to Space Force's system. Good. It would make working together much easier.

"Lieutenant Hurd, Reaper Squadron. We're pinned down on deck seven. Meeting fierce resistance. Can't make it to our fighters. Seek immediate relief," the voice said, desperation apparent. The sound of small arms fire and explosions were audible behind Hurd.

No reply except, "we're pinned down ourselves!"

Snett examined the map of the *Kentucky*, finding the fastest route to deck six. Where there had been no known attackers. "We go to deck six, follow the main north-south corridor to the intersection with the main east-west. We cut through the floor with det-tape, down the west corridor, ten bulkheads back, so as not to be noticed. We come up through deck six, hit deck seven, and smash these black armored bastards from behind. Oorah?"

"Oorah!" the whole squad returned in unison.

"We go in hot boys, no mercy. Shoot first, shoot to kill. This one's for Corporal Greck!"

12

Admiral Drex had never faced a foe who could teleport right on to his ship. From reviewing holocam footage from the initial wave of the attack he was able to conclude that the black-clad troopers were coming through wormholes. Neither Drex, nor Slaath had ever seen such advanced tech. It usually took more power to generate a wormhole than an entire capital ship could produce.

Early in the Great War, when human and drak had set the galaxy afire, the Republic had used wormholes to send missiles through. The practice was abandoned soon after it started, as it took an entire planet's worth of resources to send one missile to the Drako system. Whoever—whatever —was behind the attack, had nearly unlimited power at their disposal.

"If they can send a boarding party through worm-holes..." Slaath broke off, stroking his ceramite-plasteel alloy chin. "...perhaps they are the same ones who eat the stars themselves? Perhaps we are facing an alliance that is working with the Vargon?"

"Perhaps, Commander. Perhaps," Drex replied. He was deflated, and watched via the various cameras throughout the ship on his table's holoprojector as his crew and security teams were shredded to pieces by the superior force.

Then the ship shook, violently. With most of the pilots either tied up in close quarters combat throughout the ship, or dead already, only a handful of Spartans had been launched. Not nearly enough. A battlecruiser, two destroyers, and three frigates of Terran make, and two destroyers and two corvettes of Drakon make were pummeling the *Kentucky* with all they had. The only thing Admiral Drex had to be thankful for was they seemed to have no light fighters.

Drex had remote access to the CIC from his quarters, though with a VIP guest like Slaath aboard protocol dictated that he remain in quarters with the drak. So if comms went down command would be passed on to his first-mate, Commander Crom. As it was, comms were fine, and Drex was projected on the CIC's holoscreen.

"Ensign Gar, take us into the debris field of the fifth fleet. We've got no cover, and until we get some, the *Kentucky* is a sitting duck," he issued the order, not noticing Slaath standing behind him, nodding approval.

"Aye, aye, Admiral," the ensign said, as he punched the coordinates into the navicomputer.

They could put the bulk of a shattered destroyer, and battleship between themselves and the dark fleet bearing down on them. Drex knew it was the same fleet that had destroyed his beloved fifth. It stabbed the old man in the heart to know that the fleet he'd commanded for decades was all but gone. Tens of thousands of lives lost. Preliminary scans revealed no survivors. Drex set his jaw, as he realized the *Kentucky* was all that remained of his fleet.

A s the ship maneuvered into the debris field Drex watched as his Spartans completely destroyed one of the drakon corvettes. It was a start. "Serves the bastards right," he said, turning over his shoulder to see Slaath and Bast both watching the ship break apart. It erupted in a series of fiery explosions, before fading into so many chunks of hot metal growing ever colder.

Drex ordered his chief weapons officer to unload on the oncoming dark fleet. While it wasn't a battleship, the *Kentucky* was still one of the largest ships ever built by the Terran Republic, which meant it was one of the largest ships ever built. At least in the known history of the galaxy. It had thousands of mechanized batteries. Turbo cannons, missile batteries, anti-missile batteries, laser cannons, rail-guns that fired depleted uranium rounds, quad plasma cannon batteries...the list went on. The *Kentucky* was armed to the teeth. And the renegade fleet immediately felt the sting when it unloaded.

"All wings, this is Admiral Drex," he called out to his Spartans. "Concentrate all fire on the destroyers. Let's put more debris between us and that battlecruiser. Standard bombing run, across their battle line, then break south and RTB."

Slaath had no idea why Drex would order his Spartans

to return to the *Kentucky*, but he was curious to find out. How the Admiral's tactical mind worked was a mystery Slaath had wondered about for far too long.

Twelve of the fifteen Spartans who made it off the carrier were still in action. One was crippled, dead in the water. Floating out in empty space, with its systems shut down, hoping no enemies took notice. They wouldn't. She'd register as simple detritus from the previous battle. Two Spartans were dead, destroyed by a flurry of fire from the heavy batteries at the bow of the battlecruiser. But the other twelve lit up the destroyers with everything they still had. Plasma missiles, uranium and plutonium positron warheads, blaster cannons, rail guns, and most lethal of all—graviton bombs.

The first destroyer's shields held for the most part, but they were pushed to their limit. The second did not fare so well. By the time Shadow Three had sent his graviton payload into its hull the shields were already gone. The bulkheads crumbled, the hull smashed in on itself like a crushed soda can, as the ship's density was increased a thousand fold. It crumbled under its own weight, every crewman upon it smashed like a Baruvian melon. The Spartans broke off, heading below the ecliptic, south; as Drex had ordered. The graviton effect wore off on the smashed destroyer and it erupted in a blast that finished off the shields and obliterated the hull of the adjacent ship, just as the *Kentucky* loosed twelve torpedoes at it. When the smoke cleared Drex could see that he got his debris field.

Just as he was opening his mouth to issue the next order he heard a muffled gasp behind him. Drex spun around to see Bast coughing up blood, a vibro-blade protruding from his chest. A black-armored human trooper had appeared from nowhere. No sign, no warning, nothing other than the acrid stench of sulphur in the air. The black power armored marine flung Major Bast off his blade, but the old Croc was too stubborn to slump to the floor and die. He went to one knee, coughing up blood.

"Is that all you got?" the marine said. Then he collapsed, faceplanting on Drex's table on the way down. Still, he was breathing. Drex didn't know too much about drak anatomy, but he knew the attacker had missed Bast's heart.

Slaath became a lightning bolt of pure fury. Without fear his hand flashed out, gripping the man by the throat. His bionic eye gleamed, glowing a bright red, then discharged an energy blast that would have taken the soldier's head off had it been aimed there. But Slaath hadn't aimed at the head. He turned his gaze, and shot the man in the shoulder instead. It tore the would-be assassin's arm off in a sickening spray of blood and chunks.

The attacker dropped his vibro-sword, screamed in agony, and went to his knees. Slaath picked up the trooper's severed armored arm and beat him with it. He beat the man upon the shoulders, chest, head, and neck. Slaath slammed the arm into the attacker over and over until he was out of breath.

Drex was reluctant to touch the old lizard. So he simply cleared his throat instead. Slaath turned around, a craze over him. A kind of crazy Drex had not seen in many years. The Republic had cured shell shock centuries before, but Drex was looking into the eyes of a being with PTSD. It wasn't something he was used to, and it wasn't pretty.

"Put it down, Commander," Drex said, reminding Slaath of the importance of his station. "He's dead."

Slaath took a second to process what Drex was saying, but soon came back to reality. He'd drifted away to that far off place that Drex often went himself, and then some. As much as the admiral had grown to like the drak, he knew Slaath was batshit crazy.

Drex typed something into a datapad that was on his table. In moments his cabin door opened and a team of medi-bots entered the room. To Slaath's astonishment they took away the attacker before they took away Bast. A minute later and a hologram appeared on the table, a medi-bot with news as to the patients' conditions.

"The human will not live, even if we get him to emergency surgery immediately, Sir," the little bot said. "Major Bast is in critical condition. It will be a miracle if he makes it, though his chances are much higher at eight percent."

"Thank you, that will be all."

13

Captain Miller arrived at the hospital shortly after her fiasco with the gorthian brought so much attention her way that she practically had to buy the entire town a round. Whatever it took to keep people's mouths, and often other strange orifices, shut. She saw that the building was still sealed, with the rickety old neon sign flickering, making the place look like a closed bar more than a place of healing.

Miller rang the bell. No answer.

She rang again. Not even the door-bot.

Something wasn't right.

She used her helmet's sensors to scan for the weakest points of the structure. Miller had a roll of det-tape, saved for just such an occasion. It was easy to carry, didn't take up much room or weigh much. But it packed one hell of a punch. It was the preferred method of choice to cut through the heavy blast doors on starships.

She found the weakest spot, around the back side of the building. Miller didn't have time to mess around, so she taped out a simple three foot by three foot square on the wall. She stepped back, though only a few feet. Det-tape exploded with precision, always toward the surface it was attached to. Det-tape was great like that.

She keyed in a series on her gauntlet-mounted control pad, sending an infrared signal to the det-tape. There was a quick sizzling sound, a muffled *pop*, and when the smoke cleared a few moments later, a three by three hole in the wall. Miller went through without even bothering to scan for enemies. It had been too long since she'd eaten a meal, or had any sleep. She caught herself slipping, so she activated her helmet's lifeform detector with a few rapid precise blinks of her left eye.

It wouldn't have mattered either way. There was nothing alive in the small hospital, on the edge of the galaxy. Out on the fringe. Ten lightyears from Jeru knows where. Just bodies everywhere. Blasted apart by small arms fire for the most part, though some were sliced to pieces. A few of the dead shredded by a frag grenade.

A small fire still smoldered in one exam room, despite the overhead sprayers. The smell of fire retardant hung thick in the air. Miller switched on her exosuit's filtration unit. In moments she was breathing clean, filtered air. The filter would have kicked on automatically if the air got toxic enough, but that wasn't Miller's problem. She just didn't like the chemical smell of the fire retardant. It brought to the front of her mind a memory which she couldn't quite fully grasp. A shadow of a scar left on her mind by some long-past battle on some world whose name she no longer cared to remember. *Funny how smells can trigger such intense reactions,*

Miller thought as she scanned for Lieutenant Commander Blick, to no avail.

"Lionel, I need immediate pick-up. Everyone at the hospital is dead. Blick is gone," Miller said, deflated. "Think you can track him?"

"Roger, Captain," Lionel's voice replied over the same channel. "En route now to your location. I should be able to track Blick's ID tag."

"Good," Miller said. "If we could find out who did this, it would be a good frakkin' start."

A moment later the Spartan fighter-mech was landing just outside the hospital. Miller embarked. As soon as she strapped into the cockpit and plugged her exosuit into the neural interface Lionel gave her some bad news.

"Captain, everyone in this town seems to be converging on the spaceport. It appears to be an angry mob. There are even several lifeforms bearing actual torches," Lionel showed concern. He seemed genuinely upset. More at the degradation of civility than anything else. "The crowd seems to be worked up about a Captain Krynn. It's about to get medieval, isn't it?"

"Krynn is our ride out of here. He's who I made a deal with to get the prisoners and the bots off this rock, Lionel," Miller tried to lay it out without having to explain further.

Lionel made a sound much like a human clearing their throat when words did not suffice.

"Okay. Okay. He's a pirate," Miller admitted. "Still, our only chance of getting everyone back to the fleet. And we need to know what that drak corporal knows. As well as whatever Blick does."

"Consorting with pirates is against Republic regulations, Captain."

"Shove it, Lionel," Miller said as she keyed in an override that would keep him from giving her any lip.

"Drop me above hangar forty two. Then, I want you to suppress that mob. They are almost to the hangar, and it is imperative that Krynn not be harmed. Your orders are to shoot first, don't ask questions," Miller informed her ship of its duties. "Protect Captain Krynn and the *Banshee's Lament* at all costs, Lionel."

The F-138 Spartan came to an abrupt stop and hovered above hangar forty two. The mob was half a block away. Miller exited the ship via a drop-rope, sliding down to the hangar's roof. In that moment she was really regretting unloading everything she had at that frigate back in the Lyran system. Lionel had little left for ammo, just a couple hundred fifty cal rounds, and half a charge pack in the blaster cannon. No ordinance at all.

Lionel converted to his mech mode. A forty-foot-tall knight of the Republic, resplendent in his glory. He held his blaster canon in his left hand, and an enormous vibro-blade emanated from his right. The winged sword emblem of Shadow Squadron blazoned on the mech's shoulder gleamed in the blue-green glow of the energy sword. Lionel was ready to wreck anyone that came near the hangar. He came screaming out of the sky like an inbound meteor. Lionel's repulsors broke his fall and brought his huge frame to the ground in front of the mob just as they approached the hangar.

Taking Lionel's lead, Miller used the repulsor jets on her boots to guide herself down from the hangar roof. She landed with little more force than is she had hopped up a foot off the ground under normal circumstances. The bay doors were open, and she could see Lionel, beginning to tangle with the mob, outside. Her lifeform scanner showed that both Krynn, and his first-mate, were aboard the ship. But it also showed Miller something that pissed her off to no end. They were both asleep.

"Goddmnit!" the captain swore to herself. "Of course he's napping! What else would a grunk humping flarg tosser like Krynn be doing when an angry mob was about to beat his door down and drag him off into the street?"

"Captain Krynn! Get up! The shit's hit the fan, and the fan is your frakking doorstep!" Miller yelled over the channel they'd agreed to use.

No response. No static. Nothing. Miller was sure that his comms were all on mute as she tried channel after channel. If he didn't hear her over the general Republic civilian channels, then he didn't hear her at all.

"Does this guy ever do anything *but* disappoint?" Miller said to herself, expecting no one to answer. To her surprise, Lionel chimed in.

"Toss a frag grenade. Throw it right on top of his ship. It won't breach the hull, but it should get anyone's attention who is inside," the mech offered as it began to chop through the crowd with the vibro-blade. A massive scythe through a field of wheat.

The crowd was a cantankerous roar. A beast with two hundred mouths, all screaming for blood. Then the shoulder mounted fifty-cal machine gun spat hot death, its bursts drowning out the crowd. Lionel turned to his blaster cannon next, spending the magazine in seconds, creating several smoking craters in the street. In a moment, the last of the mech's ammo gone, and the mob kept coming. With only CQC weapons there was little he could do to stem the tide of ruffians, bandits, and thugs who swarmed toward the hangar.

Miller had two frag grenades. She threw the first on top of Krynn's ship, just as Lionel had suggested. It thumped against the hull with a deafening *crack!* Then she tossed her last frag out onto the street, just as the first of the mob who'd made it past her forty-foot killing machine came at the hangar door. Five of them went splat, and then Miller was raining hot death from her blaster. Each time she fired, a blue-hot energy blast took at least one life. Her helmet's systems tagged targets and displayed them on her HUD while her exosuit guided her hand to take them out with a rapidity and precision that bordered on prescience.

More of the mob of random aliens fell to her blaster than to Lionel's thirty foot vibro-sword. A distinctive yawning sound came over her helmet's speakers. Miller was more annoyed than relieved, and then Lionel's shoulder exploded. Shattered by a depleted uranium rocket fired from a shoulder mounted launcher. His sword arm twitched as it dangled by a few wires before tearing itself off and smashing to the ground.

The mob felt emboldened, as dozens of blaster rifles, laser rifles, and slug throwers opened up on the mech. Overwhelmed, Lionel took a step backward. He stumbled on a heap of dead aliens as a second rocket connected with his head, blowing it into a thousand pieces. The mech smashed about with its massive blaster cannon, crushing several of the aliens directly in front of it, just out of sheer luck. As they swarmed past the fighter-mech, one of the random howling creatures of the pack, a cryxian pirate, placed a det-pack on Lionel's leg. It didn't detonate in a large, fiery explosion. Which would have been great for Miller as it would have taken many aliens with it. No. It caused a small *pop*, but created such extreme heat in such a small area that the leg gave way completely, toppling the mech onto its side. The mob swarmed over it, tearing Lionel apart with picks and vibro-axes. *Primitives*, Miler thought.

Syn Miller's blaster barked, *br-rak br-rak br-rak*, in five round bursts. More of the onslaught fell. And for every one to die it seemed like two more took its place. There were more of them on the Lyran moon than scans had suggested. Still, even as she killed them with ruthless efficiency, Miller felt in her gut that none of them had anything to do with what had happened at the hospital. They probably just wanted to collect the bounty on Krynn, now that they knew there was one. Plus every thug on every backwater rock in the galaxy wanted to be able to brag about offing a Space Force officer. Pilot, marine, soldier. It didn't matter. When the lowest of the low get a chance to destroy the elite of the elite, they take the chance. And that goes for anywhere in the galaxy.

Even on a forgotten moon on the fringe street cred meant something.

"Miller? Is that you out there? Seems to be some sort of commotion. Hold yer horses," Krynn finally responded.

"Let me in, Krynn! I'm about to be overrun here, and

they've just destroyed my Spartan!" Miller yelled at him with as much venom in her voice as she could manage. Her rifle's charge was getting dangerously low. And she knew that if she stopped to reload she'd be overrun.

Miller fell back from her position, close to the bay door. It had cover behind a mechanic's forklift, and a good view of the street…and the oncoming alien horde. Nearly overrun, Miller found herself in the open, running for her life toward the *Banshee's Lament*.

And the boarding ramp should be lowering. Except it's not.

And Krynn should be providing covering fire. Except he's not.

Syn Miller was alone, and beginning to panic, despite her training. Despite all the conditioning and implants to regulate her heart rate, emotions, hormonal response, and other functions. Despite her cybernetic upgrades and the nano-bots that kept her mind and body calm and healthy, Miller began to panic.

"Let me the frak in Krynn!" Miller screamed, desperate for her life. A quick glance at her blaster's charge told her that all full force her M-85 had ten rounds left. She switched over to half force. It would still be deadly at close enough range, but gave her twenty shots.

And she used them all. And Krynn still hadn't opened the ramp. A slug slammed into her shoulder. Miller chanced a quick glance and saw that it had not penetrated her armor.

"Krynn! Let me in, I AM ABOUT TO DI…" Miller didn't get to finish her sentence.

The *Lament* engaged its vertical takeoff engines, and

hovered five feet off the ground. The hangar had a large enough hole in the roof, so that ships could take off and land directly from it, though the hole accounted for less than half the total area of the massive roof. It was standard issue that way, and Miller was thankful.

The *Lament's* engines kicked up enough dust and debris that a thick cloud filled the hangar and billowed out the bay doors. Miller could still see as she set her helmet to filter out the dust. One of the perks of being in Space Force.

The pirates, smugglers, and thugs out in the street were overwhelmed by the cloud. Miller heard the strange sounds of many aliens choking and coughing.

"Sorry, Miller. I had to hang the hog a little...you know how it is. Anyway, I have a bad pneumatic actuator on my boarding ramp. Sorry I couldn't let you in. Your suit got jump-jets? Can you get to the top of the *Lament?* There's a hatch up top, and Lemmy's waiting to let you in."

"Uh, yeah. I've got one jump's worth of charge left," Miller said as she ran to the ship, leapt into the air, and kicked on her exosuit's booster jets. It was just enough to get her to the top of the ship.

""You make it up?" Krynn yelled, just as the mob poured into the hangar. The cloud had subsided enough to see.

"Yeah, I'm here. I see the hatch. And the lyran is waving at me. See you in a sec..." Miller affirmed.

And then the *Banshee's Lament* unleashed hell on the mob. Two mini-gun pods dropped from the bottom of its hull, and a grenade launcher from just beneath the cockpit, and they all opened up at once. One mini-gun would have been plenty. Two was more than sufficient, bordering on cruelty. And the grenade launcher was total overkill.

Within three seconds there was nothing left of anything coming through the bay doors. And the walls of the hangar began to cave. As the *Lament* shot straight up into the night sky and out over the desert, the entire building collapsed on the remaining few fighters.

"There, you see? All dead," Krynn said, pleased with himself, as Miller entered the cockpit.

He turned a monitor screen so that she could see it. No signs of life at the hangar. "There had to have been hundreds of them," he said, as a cocky smile broke across his face. "Good thing I was there to save your ass, Captain." Krynn broke into laughter.

Miller sat in one of the backseat chairs, took her helmet off and placing it into one of the other empty chairs. Lemmy came in and took the copilot's seat.

"Krynn, here's the coordinates to my prisoner and bots. We need to stop for them," Miller said as she pulled up a map on her wrist's holoprojector. With a flick of her finger she sent the map to the *Lament's* navicomputer.

"What happened to the other guy? The one in the hospital?" Krynn asked, showing what passed for genuine concern. "Wasn't he important?"

"He's not on the planet anymore. It's like he got snatched right through a wormhole."

"He did. That's exactly what happened. They call themselves the *Coalition*. The same guys you tangled with out there," Krynn motioned out the viewport, at empty space. "They work for the Vargon Empire, and intend to be the kings who reign over the ashes after the galaxy burns."

"Wha—what did you say, Krynn?" Miller flew into a panic induced rage. She had never mentioned the Vargon to him. The lyran laughed. Through its tusked mouth, it came out as a strange snarling sound.

"I said, welcome to Void Ops, Captain. You're whole world has changed."

14

XJ-13 held the blaster pistol on the drak corporal while Kevin scanned the surrounding area for incoming hostiles, or signs of Captain Miller's return. XJ had never imagined that he'd be holding a blaster on someone. After all, he was a medi-bot. A healer. He was programmed to do no harm. But a Space Force captain's orders could supersede his programming at any time, galactic security at stake or not.

Kevin kept reminding XJ-13 that if they really wanted to help the Republic, as was their programming, they would torture the drak corporal until Captain Miller returned. And XJ refused. The conversation went on for over an hour, in Kevin's bot speech. The drak didn't understand the language, but both bots knew he was aware of the subject matter. His respiration, heart rate, pupil dilation, and general uneasiness made that apparent.

Corporal Fenn wondered how long it would take them to make a decision, decided he didn't care, and curled up in the escape pod and went to sleep. It might be the last good rest he ever got, at least for a long while, if they didn't execute him. Kevin was reminding XJ-13 that holding a blaster on the captive drak was the most heroic thing the medi-bot had ever done when a ship showed up on their scanners. A fast moving ship. And it wasn't a Republican Spartan.

"Whatever it is, KV-1N it is heading right for us," XJ-13 said, stating the obvious. A pet peeve of Kevin's.

The slicer-bot issued a series of beeps and blips. Rocking back and forth on its repulsors, exaggerating its gestures for emphasis.

"What do you mean that it is a Republic ship?" XJ-13 asked. "I've never heard of *Void Ops*. Stop making things up you sentient waste-bin."

Another series of beeps. The shelled dome that served as Kevin's head spun in place as he discharged steam from his ports. Kevin turned away and watched the ship approach as its landing struts began to deploy.

"How very rude!" XJ-13 replied. "It isn't my fault I wasn't programmed with knowledge of every aspect of Republic special operations. I was created for use in Republic Navy infirmaries. Not for spy missions on the backwater worlds at the edge of the galaxy."

Kevin didn't reply. The little bot chose to make XJ feel dumber than it already did. Just a light chuckle. Of course XJ-13 was resentful. He wasn't a member of the most elite intelligence outfit in the galaxy, nor did he have a direct sub-space line to the Office of the Chancellor of the Republic, the OCR. The cost of a Spartan fighter-mech was only half of the cost of an espionage bot like KV-1N.

But there was hardly a way for the littler bot to bring it up without sounding like an elitist.

The ship landed less than fifty yards from the escape pod. XJ-13 scanned his memory banks and found that he did indeed have a file on the vessel. A Great War era light cruiser once thought lost at the battle of Dorn, the *Banshee's Lament*. A warship from a time when the Republic was at war. The statement, "they don't make 'em like they used to," seemed an understatement to XJ-13. It caused him no small amount of consternation that the ship was being ID'd as a pirate vessel. Whoever owned it now, was not a hero of the Republic.

Captain Miller exited the boarding ramp of the *Banshee's Lament*, M-85 at the ready. She had a glazed over look to her eyes, and by the dirt, grime, blood, and gore caked to her armor the bots could see that she'd been through quite a lot since they'd seen her. When she was within ten yards of the escape pod she whistled as loudly as she could without her helmet's vox amplification system.

"Bots, load up on the *Lament* over there," she motioned with the barrel of her blaster rifle toward the ship. "I'll get the prisoner."

"Did Lieutenant Commander Blick make it, Captain?" XJ-13 asked. "I did not detect him aboard the ship."

"I don't know, bot. Maybe, maybe not," Captain Miller said, shaking her head in disbelief. "Either way, someone came and took him while I was busy hiring Captain Krynn. Load up, we're moving out, now."

Miller didn't watch as the bots headed toward the ship

and up the loading ramp. She didn't listen to anything that XJ-13 had to say, though she knew that there was plenty more of it. *Damn bot could talk the balls off a pachysaurus*, she thought. The sound of her own voice resounded in her head, and further drowned out any of the bot's concerns that apathy had not already.

"Corporal Fenn, wake up, now!" Miller yelled at the drak.

He snored. "ZZZZ…"

She walked into the pod, stood over Fenn and gave him a swift kick in the ribs. Her HUD let her know that she broke two of his ribs the moment her boot connected with him. The drak yelped, rising up off the ground from the force of the blow.

"Wha—?" he gasped.

"Get up, you slug. We're leaving," Miller said as she leveled her M-85 at the young drak. "Now!"

She discharged a blast, scorching the control panel on the hull behind him. The pod filled with the smell of ozone as a small electrical fire broke out. Miller knew she had the lizardman's attention, and in that moment was more than thankful that Krynn had given her a fresh magazine.

Reluctantly, he got to his feet, and marched to the *Lament*. It took much longer than Miller would have liked to load everyone up on the ship. For some reason, Kevin kept coming back down the ramp and scanning the sky, which made Fenn stare up and stumble more than once. Miller chanced a glance up herself, but saw nothing. She was the last one up the ramp, which apparently had no problems at all with the pneumatic actuators. When she boarded Miller found Krynn was already interrogating the drak in the common area. Both were sitting at a holochess table, Lemmy stood behind Fenn with a blaster pistol on the drak.

"So Fenn, you're Coalition. I get it. You want the ashes of the galaxy to yourselves. But see us…we don't want the galaxy to burn. We don't want some stuck up grunk humping phase three civilization to take everything we've built over millennia without a fight," Krynn leaned in close, staring the corporal hard in the eyes. He imparted a seriousness that Miller had yet to see. She found it exciting. Dangerous. She quickly reminded herself that he could probably pull out any one of a dozen personalities at the drop of a hat. After all, he was a spy. A spy for the most clandestine organization in the entire Terran Republic.

The drak said nothing. Miller was getting impatient to depart. The drak corporal could wait. Krynn drew his own blaster pistol from the holster on his right thigh. An LN-93. Fenn's eyes widened. A blaster rarely seen throughout the galaxy, the Krupp Armstech LN-93 could take the head off a fully armored drak space marine heavy at close range. There would be no surviving a blast from it. Even one to the arm, or leg would likely prove fatal.

"Look, Fenn," Krynn plead with the drak. "I'd just as soon dust you right here, and have one of these bots clean up what's left of you, as I would hear a lie from your filthy Coalition mouth. Now, spill everything you've got. If I so much as suspect a lie, I'll toast your reptoid ass. Got me?"

"I've nothing to say to you. To none of you," the drak said as he turned to face Miller. "There's nothing the Coalition won't do to me if I talk to you."

"Too bad," Krynn said as he stood up. He started walking to the ship's cockpit, turned over his shoulder and gave the boar-headed lyran, Lemmy, a quick gesture. The lyran dragged the drak through the ship by the left arm. He was much stronger and it was as if a small child were dragging around a much larger doll. When they got to the airlock the drak began to weep. One look from Lemmy and Fenn quieted down. It was a look that promised much more pain if the drak failed to be compliant.

Miller's boots automatically mag-sealed to the deck as the ship ascended into the clouds of the moon. She thought it was a great idea to make the drak think that they would eject him into the coldness of space, or even the upper atmosphere. It was a fate that none wanted to meet, a fate much worse than being blasted. Even by an LN-93.

When the *Banshee's Lament* entered the uppermost reaches of the Lyran moon's atmosphere Krynn's voice came over the ship's general PA system. "Now, Lemmy."

The lyran kicked the drak in the chest hard. The blow knocked Fenn back into the airlock. Lemmy then slammed his fist on the control panel, which closed Fenn into the airlock door and secured the hatch. He walked over to the adjacent controls. A small rectangular panel surrounded with black and yellow chevrons, with dozens of flashing lights and various buttons and switches. But only one large, red button behind a security switch. The drak banged on the door out of desperation as Lemmy armed the airlock.

Miller still thought that Krynn was playing the drak, trying to get him to spill his guts about the Coalition. She was shocked when the first-mate simply hit the bright red eject button, blasting a prisoner of war into space, without even thinking twice.

M iller stormed into the luxurious cockpit of the *Lament*. She was furious. Not because of any loyalty to her prisoner, but because everything was on the line. It was the Republic itself that would pay the price for what Krynn did with a prisoner, which technically, had been hers.

"You spaced my prisoner, Krynn! What the frak where you thinking, you asshat?" Miller screamed. "There's no excuse for that."

"Calm down, Miller. He didn't know anything that we don't already. He was a liability. I don't have a secure place to keep an enemy on this vessel," Krynn seemed dismissive as he punched in hyperspace coordinates into his navigation computer.

"What do you mean, *calm down?*" Miller asked, ready to draw her weapon on Krynn. Just when she'd started to give him the benefit of the doubt.

"I mean, I have tech you wouldn't even believe existed if I showed it to you yesterday. KV-1N...Kevin, he is my bot. He's been deep undercover for Void Ops for months now," Krynn paused as if Miller were supposed to be impressed. He gave her his toothy, rakish smile and it made her a little sick. It was the smile of a used hover-car salesman on a backwater planet.

"What does Kevin have to do with Fenn?" Miller asked.

"He took a complete neural scan of the drak when it was in the escape pod. Everything it knew, everything it ever thought, is all available to us as a holofile. A neutrino scanner, KV-1N has one. Some of the best tech in the galaxy. Scanned that drak's entire existence in seconds and he never knew it. Kevin's interfacing with the *Lament's* quantum computer systems to track down any relevant information in the file that we'll just call *Fenn* now. Thank you very much!" Krynn ended, very pleased with himself.

He punched the hyperdrive, it engaged, and they slingshot out of real-space and into hyperspace. Miller only then realized that she didn't know where they were going, and that if it weren't the *Kentucky* she had no control over it. As a newly recruited member of Void Ops her new mission would probably supersede her command of Shadow Squadron.

"A neutrino scanner?" Miller asked. It was all she could think to do.

"Yeah. We get the most advanced tech available to any Terran citizen, civilian or military. Void Ops perk. Even arcane tech, alien tech, banned tech, suppressed tech... Heretical stuff for the most part. Things the average citizen, or even soldier, is better off not knowing exist," Krynn said. He got quite serious and Miller knew this was a subject close to him. She thought for a moment she saw the true Felo Krynn, beneath all the personas and tradecraft. She thought she saw a nerd who liked to geek out about gadgets, and for the first time since she'd left the *Kentucky*, Miller felt comfortable.

"So, do I get an upgrade to my security clearance, or what?" Miller smiled as she asked. "I was already a G-11…"

Krynn interrupted her, "check your status over the Republic Space Force fleet database."

Miller punched a few keystrokes into her gauntlet's keypad. A moment later and her jaw dropped. "It says I'm KIA. Dead since the Battle of Lyra. I see…"

"Syn Miller is dead. She no longer exists. Unless you don't want the mission…"

"No, Captain Krynn. I'm on board. Whatever it takes to save the Republic," Miller was sincere, and imparted as much with her tone. "I've never been one to dismiss the call of duty."

"Which is precisely why you are standing here right now," Krynn said, giving her a reassuring smile. "I know you will get the job done, no matter how dirty it is. And I know you will give everything for the Republic, and now it needs you more than ever. You're one of the last real true believers out there, and believe me, I spent months combing through the files of Space Force personnel for this mission."

"Thank you, Sir. I won't let you down. Now, what is the mission?"

"We're going to New Terra."

"New Terra! It's been too long since I've been home," Miller said, reminiscence in her voice. She was on the edge of getting choked up.

"Don't get too excited. We're not going home to sight see. And we ain't going on vacation."

"Will you just spill it, Krynn? Enough with the antici-pation. What will we be there to do?" she said. Miller was nervous, though excited.

"We're going to assassinate Chancellor Krell."

15

Sergeant Snett led his men down the corridor, onto the lift and onto deck six. He had no idea just how big the *Kentucky* was until he found himself running down its corridors. The plan was simple. Cut through the ceiling with a cutting torch, climb into the seventh deck, kick the enemy's ass from behind. Then the Space Force pilots who were pinned down could make it to their fighters. Snett just hoped that Reaper Squadron was still alive by the time they got there.

No signs of life. Scanners gave the team the signal to move. But sometimes electronic devices are wrong. And sometimes specially trained operatives lose focus in the heat of the moment and lean too hard on such devices. This was one of those times.

Snett and his men rounded a bulkhead into the main corridor, a straight shot to their objective. They were surprised to see two black armored troopers before them. The drakon marines were too slow to react and the troopers opened up on them with G-2 blasters. Lance

Corporal Bekk, Private C'lar, and Private Trell were dusted before the marines could return fire.

Snett shoved the man behind him, Private Gorn, back with his left hand while he blasted away at the dark troopers with his rifle. A stray blast scorched the bulkhead behind Snett, and Gorn was thankful that the Sergeant shoved him back. His head would have caught the blast. Snett charged straight at the troopers, whose armor was as resilient as any Space Force marine's. As blaster bolts scorched their obsidian shells the black clad troopers were too disoriented by the firestorm to return fire accurately, and Snett closed the distance with ease.

As soon as he was upon them he beat the first over the head with his rifle butt and drew his combat knife. A wicked vibro-blade, curved in the style of the drakon, that hummed a low buzz as Snett slashed at the second. The man he clubbed crumpled to the ground. Though his helmet was still intact, the insurgent was knocked out completely. The second struggled to block Snett's thrusts and jabs with his own rifle. He managed to catch the blade of the vibro-knife in the trigger guard and wrench it away from Snett, though it destroyed his trigger, leaving his weapon useless as a blaster.

As the trooper in black realized the damage done to his rifle a blaster fired from behind Snett and shattered the faceplate of his helmet. He slumped forward, dead. Of the ten marines who'd departed the landing shuttle, only six remained. Snett gave a nod of approval to Gorn, who'd shot the second trooper.

"We'll mourn our dead later. We have a mission to accomplish now. Men, let's move," Snett said to his squad.

"Be ready for anything. You see something, and it doesn't show as friendly on your HUD, you dust it. No more surprises. They can come from anywhere, and we need to adapt to that...yesterday."

The marines moved down the rest of deck six's corridor unopposed. But they wondered how long it would be before the two they'd just offed were discovered, along with the bodies of the three drakon marines who died in the exchange. Chances were, it wouldn't be long, and they all knew it. A sense of urgency overcame the squad.

"If the *Kentucky* can't launch its fighters, then we're all dead anyway. Oorah?" Snett asked his men to confirm his notion.

"Oorah, Sarge," Gorn returned, as he stood over-watch while Tegg and Brinn cut through the ceiling with a plasma torch.

"What I wouldn't give for a roll of Republic det-tape," Tegg said. "It is going to take us a few more minutes before we get through."

"Roger that," Snett replied. Then he switched over to Republic comms, which made a lump come into his throat. He knew it wasn't the time to get nervous and swallowed hard with an exaggerated gulp. "Reaper Squadron, you still there?"

"Yeah, and are we glad to hear from you!" a young voice answered. "What's your ETA, Sarge? We're pinned down, the CO's dead. But we're still in the fight."

Snett could hear blaster fire in the background, followed by the concussive *crak!* of a frag grenade. From the sound of it the fighting was fierce on the seventh deck.

"We're a couple minutes out. Coming up from the

sixth floor behind the enemy position. You should be reading us on your scanners…"

"Got ya. Ok, we see six of you. There's six of us too, all that remains of Reaper Squadron. I'm in charge…now. Lieutenant Colt," the young man said. Snett could tell he was nervous, and probably hadn't been in a firefight in a very long time, if ever.

"Sarge, we're through," Gorn said. A moment later and a loud crash shook the deck as the chunk of ceiling fell to the floor.

"Ok, Colt. We're coming up now. Take cover. And whatever you do, don't shoot us. That's all I'm asking. Now, kill the bastards!" Sergeant Snett yelled as Tegg went through the breach, boosted up by Gorn.

The last one up was Snett, who watched his men's backs as they ascended, each pulled up by the preceding man. They found themselves at the lonely end of a long corridor. At the other end, fifty meters away, what remained of Reaper Squadron was hunkered down behind a barricade made of a shattered bulkhead, some cargo palettes, two smashed work-bots, and several dead bodies in power armor. Some Republic Space Force, some the black-clad troopers.

In the middle of the corridor were a dozen enemy troopers trying to take cover wherever they cold find it. They were concentrating fire on Reaper Squadron with a heavy blaster team while the others advanced from bulkhead to bulkhead. The heavy blaster, a Lockheed MG-57, was laying down so much fire the Spartans couldn't even get a shot off. The dark troopers were too caught up in the moment to check their scanners, or they would have realized they were shadowed by the drak marines.

Snett motioned for his men to move forward and take firing positions. All six marines picked two targets and locked them. Then on Snett's signal their blasters barked *br-rak! br-rak!* Three of the troopers died instantly, their armor failing to provide protection from the AI assisted aim of the marines. Three more were critically wounded and taken out of the fight, dying slowly and painfully.

Six remained. Four armed with blaster rifles and the two-man heavy blaster team. The MG-57 continued to harry the pilots while the other four troopers turned on the marines, who peppered them with a withering storm of fire. Somehow the squad leader of the black troopers was able to engage a device that provided a shimmering energy field around each of his men. Only one fell to the drakon blaster fire before the energy shield absorbed all the damage intended for them.

"Frak this," Snett said, as he pulled the massive sixty-calibre slug thrower on his hip. "I haven't seen shields like those ever in my life, but I bet they won't stop this!"

Snett charged down the corridor, a mad lizard, frothing at the mouth. His HUD told him that his action took the men by surprise as he unleashed round after round from his slug thrower. His own armor was shredded under the four troopers' blaster fire as he took the lead one right between the eyes. The trooper's ceramite-plasteel helmet shattered by the force of the solid lead slug. Snett was right, the solid round went right through the energy shield. Just like most of them, it only stopped energy weapons.

One down, the other three continued to blast at Snett, who in his rage felt none of it. He snatched the closest man by the throat and blasted him right through the chest with the slug thrower. The round tore right through the mechanized exosuit, spraying blood across Snett's helmet. Snett lost sight, with his HUD's camera's all covered in gore. He heaved the dead trooper out of his hand and onto the heavy blaster team, toppling them and their weapon. But as he did so one of the troopers slipped his gun barrel under Snett's guard and opened up on the lizardman's neck.

A plug of flesh was zapped right off the Sergeant. A fist sized chunk where his shoulder met his throat. But he didn't notice in the moment. He lashed about in his blindness, determined to land a blow on one of the remaining troopers.

"Sarge! Get down!" Gorn screamed as he rushed the troopers with his vibro-knife ready, blasting them with his rifle. The rest of the marines followed, and the members of Reaper Squadron poured out from behind their makeshift cover, charging with knives, rifles, pistols, and in one case bare hands.

The marines tore into the troopers as a rabid limcat tears into a baby. Sergeant Snett fell to the ground, his legs going out from under him as he got light headed from loss of blood. His HUD informed him that he was dying, and that he had only moments to live, as it pumped him full of a cocktail of painkilling drugs to make him comfortable on his transition to the other side. The last thing he heard was the muffled screams of the final black-clad trooper being torn apart limb from limb by his men.

16

"You can't be serious. I mean…why? Is he with this Coalition?" Miller asked. She bit her lip, chewed it slightly. A habit she'd had since she was a teenager, all those hundreds of cycles ago. "If he's a traitor, sure. I'll knock him off, and call it a day. But you've got to realize…"

"Gotcha!" Krynn laughed. "No, we aren't needed on New Terra. Not yet. And no, we aren't hitting the frakkin' chancellor," he laughed some more, turning red in the face. Lemmy snorted, the closest thing his lyran anatomy could do to laughing.

"So what *are* we doing then, Captain?" Miller said, annoyance heavy in her words. "Does the fleet really think I'm dead?"

"No. It was just a glitch. When you booted back up it should have patched you back in to the network. Once it registered your vitals and noticed you are alive," Krynn said, growing serious. "We're headed for the Lahkmar system. We have a date with the Vargon themselves, if my source is to be trusted. And she's never once failed me."

"The Vargon? We're going to meet them?" Miller glanced about the cabin. She bit her lip again.

"No. We are going to record them doing what they do best. Devouring a system. We need to learn everything about them that we can. My agent within the Coalition gave me the Lahkmar system as the next target of their appetite," Krynn explained.

Miller pondered just what it is that they were doing and wondered if the Republic might be better served with her back in the cockpit of an F-138 Spartan. But the thought of flying made her think of Shadow Squadron, and of Lieutenant Tova.

Miller had been out of her exosuit for hours and hadn't had any emotion stabilizing drugs pumped into her system in as long. Thick beads of tears ran in steady streams down her cheeks at the thought of her wingman. The woman could outdrink any Spartan pilot, or marine for that matter, in the fleet. A brilliant historian of Old Terran military tactics, from before the invention of the hyperdrive, Tova loved to talk about ancient wars. From the time when soldiers fought with spear and shield, sword and axe. But that was all that Miller really knew about Tova, other than she was one hell of a card player.

And so Miller faded into her own sadness aboard the *Banshee's Lament*. She was lost down the rabbit hole of could haves and would haves. Of one more times and of what might have beens. She didn't notice that Krynn got a priority alpha call from OCR.

A few minutes later Krynn sat beside Miller in her

cabin, wiped tears from her cheeks, and said, "I just got a sub-space call from the chancellor himself. The Coalition has managed to destroy most of the fleets still loyal to the Republic. A handful of ships from the remains of surviving fleets have banded together to defend New Terra. We are to complete our mission as planned, after which we are ordered to assist the *Kentucky* and whatever else remains of the Fifth Fleet. You'll get to go home, Miller. For a minute at least."

"What? The fleet? The Coalition?" Miller shook her head in disagreement. "This can't be happening. This can't be real."

"It is. And the news gets worse. Much worse," Felo Krynn said. He tried to show her some compassion by squeezing her hand in his. "The Confederation has fractured. More than sixty percent of its navy has joined the Coalition, and of the rest…very few remain."

"Yeah, I escorted Commander Slaath aboard the *Kentucky*. I barely got him there safely when the Coalition attacked us. Or at least the drakon branch of it. We assumed it was either a trap set *for* Slaath, or a trap set *by* him. Had we known then that they had human allies…" Miller choked back another wave of tears. "My wingman, Hellcat, didn't make it."

"I'm sorry to hear that, Syn," Captain Krynn was genuinely sincere. "But I need you to listen to me. We are going to be the ones that save this frakkin' galaxy. Why? Because no one else will. Because no one else can. Because the Republic and the Confederation both fell apart and someone needs to remain standing to glue the pieces back together."

It was just the sort of motivational speech that she needed to hear. The same kind of speech she was famous for giving herself. *Pick yourself up by your bootstraps, Syn*. She told herself.

They emerged from hyperspace a couple hours later. Miller had gotten her emotions in check, and had even played a game of holochess with Lemmy and XJ-13. She was clear headed and ready to kick ass. And then it came on the scanners. A thing of such enormous proportions that it dominated the entire system. A gargantuan, snake-like tube that extended several billion kilometers. Innumerable small drones swarmed about it, smashing any astroids, debris, space rocks, even dust particles with energy beams. Miller watched in awe as a dozen drones destroyed an astroid in less than a minute.

"Every single atom gets consumed, and recycled. They absorb everything into that giant snake. Watch this part..." Krynn pointed at the holoscreen they all watched on.

As the snake approached a planet, a gas-giant five Terran astronomical units from the system's star, thousands of hexagonal plates poured forth from its green glowing maw. Golden hexagons kilometers across. They surrounded the planet, and thousands more plates exited the snake's mouth to join them. They poured out of it until they had completely blanketed the world, and remained equidistant from one another. Great arcing beams of blue-white lightning erupted from each corner of each plate and connected them all in a spiderweb network that pulsed rippling energy across its surface.

"This is the part we've all been waiting for," Krynn said. The crew did not respond, all fixated on the screen. Only a single beep from Kevin that went unnoticed.

The Vargon plates converged on one another, eventually coming together and completely encasing the gas-giant. A few moments passed and the hexagons began to disperse. Through the gaps between the plates the crew noticed that the planet was gone.

"They took it to their pocket dimension. There the entire planet will be devoured, stripped down, and every single atom recycled into something else. They usually leave the gas-giants alone and strip rocky worlds for their carbon and metals, especially their cores. This is unprecedented," Krynn said. "This is the first documented case of this."

The ship's holoscreen switched to a view of the Lahkmar sun. It was surrounded by the snake at the equator, and a second one entered the system from hyperspace and locked into the first at a perpendicular. Both snakes dispersed their armadas of hexagonal plates, and in minutes the star was surrounded in a shell. The snake-like structures lit up with a series of pulses. Various colored lights strobing throughout the system dominating vessels. Then they began rotating gyroscopically, the golden hexagons keeping constant position with them. Moments later the entire structure disappeared, jumping out of our reality. The star was gone. The Vargon structures were gone. All the hexagons were gone, and the planets, moons, asteroids, and comets of the system went flying off on their tangential trajectories. Without the star's gravitational effect to keep them in orbit they were lost in the vast blackness.

"And that is what a Vargon attack is like. It should give us all some perspective on why the Coalition thinks they are unbeatable. Give us some perspective on why they think like they do. And why Fleet Admiral Valdana betrayed the Republic to form it. They believe they can work with the Vargon, to somehow appease them, or possibly serve them. They seek to rule over the ruins of a dead galaxy. But when the Vargon are done feasting, there will be no galaxy," Krynn spoke with venom in his voice. Disdain for Valdana apparent.

"I assumed they were woking under some sort of agreement with the Vargon. Are you telling me that they are just *hoping* that if they are loyal...." Miller was incensed. Her cheeks went flush and her pupils dilated. She began to pop her knuckles.

"Precisely, Syn. They betrayed everything humanity has been building for seventy-five-hundred cycles for a hope and a prayer," Krynn shook his head in disgust. "Do you think the yeast in a piece of bread hopes it can work with you before you bite into a sandwich?"

""That is absurd, Captain Krynn," XJ-13 chimed in, as if his opinion was wanted. "Yeast is a..."

"Oh, can it, XJ. He was using a metaphor, you buckethead," Miller said. She hated arguing with robots, but once again found herself doing just that.

"I just meant, XJ, that to the Vargon we are no more than yeast is to us. What we want, what we try to do, our motivations, policies, all that...it's meaningless, bot. Absolutely meaningless," Krynn said. He didn't share Miller's reservations about robots, and often enjoyed their stubborn obstinance simply for the chances it afforded him to have good, meaningful arguments.

Miller and Krynn went to the cockpit and set course for the Thurian system while Lemmy went to his cabin and took a nap. It wasn't too long of a jump from where they were, and Miller noticed that the Lament's hyperdrive seemed to be special. It got the ship places much faster than anything she had ever seen. She wondered if it was some of that badass alien tech that Krynn had mentioned that was to blame.

When Krynn punched the controls, the hyperdrive engaged, and reality dissolved around them. Miller found herself in that all too familiar place, watching as the stars streaked by like spaghetti strands. Faster than light travel had always boggled her mind, but it seemed so simple at that moment. Especially compared to the Vargon. *What kind of being needs to eat stars to survive?* Miller asked herself.

"What do they look like?" Miller asked. "The Vargon."

"We don't know. Not for sure. There are various unsubstantiated reports, theories, models, suppositions, myths. But nobody really knows for sure. Not yet at least," Krynn said. "But what we do know…the draks used to worship them as gods. They did so for thousands of years before they were even a spacefaring race. In recent times though, they have been disregarded as simply ancient mythology. Though, obviously, that is starting to change."

"It makes sense. Ancient star-vampire gods of the draks return and the whole galaxy is frakked," Miller said.

Her cheeks were flush again, and she found herself with clenched fists and white knuckles.

"But, here's the real treat, Miller. Kevin just completed the neutrino scan data mining project I put him on. The drak corporal's brain scans," Krynn said, impressed with himself. "The mantids have a weapon that may just do us some good. We'll need to examine the file, but if what Kevin says is true, then we need to get our hands on it, no matter the cost."

"Captain, how can that be?" Miller asked, consternation showing in the lines of her face. "The mantid race was annihilated by Space Force. There was not a single survivor on the planet of Mantalar, other than draks and humans. It was one of the worst things the Republic ever did. But the genocide of the mantids prevented another war between the humans and the draks from breaking out, so the historians will tell you it was all worth it."

"It was," Krynn tried to reassure her.

"Tell that to my father. He made the call to use the bioweapon that wiped them out."

"Ok. Two things. First, not every member of their race was on Mantalar at the time of the genocide. Their race did only have one world it called home, but they were…are, spacefaring. Their last remaining ship they call the *Ark*," Krynn said, watching a smile of relief come over Miller's face. A smile that gave way to pure joy. "And second, you can tell that to your father yourself when we get to the *Kentucky*. We're going to need every bit of help we can get in dealing with the mantids."

"So, the universe saving agenda is rendezvous with the *Kentucky*. Meet the Vargon defector. Meet the mantids and either buy, trade, or take their doomsday weapon. And lastly, use it against the Vargon," Miller stated as sarcastically as she could.

"What? You aren't down for the mission?" Krynn deadpanned. "Don't forget, we still have to deal with the Coalition, restore authority to the Republic and Confederation, and bring Fleet Admiral Valdana and the other traitors to justice. Which in Void Ops means a hot blaster up their…"

"How much does this job pay again?" Miller joked, just happy to know she was going home. Back to the *Kentucky*.

S hadow Squadron regrouped behind the cover of the shattered Republic destroyer *Eisenhower*. The bombing run they'd enacted across the dark fleet's battle-line had a devastating effect on the enemy's morale. More than simply destroying several enemy vessels, the detritus and wreckage provided more essential cover for the *Kentucky*. As per Admiral Drex's orders the Squadron began its return to the battleship.

And when the squadron was clear of the carrier's line of fire the *Kentucky* lit up the enemy battleship with as many ship to ship positron missiles as it could launch. From starboard one hundred and twenty missile batteries prepared to launch four hundred and eighty anti-matter rounds. Admiral Drex's voice came over the squadron comms.

"Shadow Squadron, follow our ordinance in for the kill. Make sure as many payloads are delivered as possible. You're job is to knock out their anti-missile defense systems. If we can knock out that battleship, we might win this fight."

It was standard procedure. Launch a salvo of homing missiles to take the brunt of their anti-missile defense systems. Followed by the heavy ordinance, assisted by a squadron of Spartans. With Miller and Tova gone the squadron command fell to Lieutenant Germana, callsign Shakedown.

"Roger that, *Kentucky*," Germana replied. "We'll give 'em the ole one two."

Shadow Squadron made a wide arcing turn in unison, keeping tight formation beneath the hull of the *Kentucky*, and pushed their ion engines to the limits of what they could do. In moments they caught up with the anti-matter ordinance as it careened toward the enemy battleship. The deck lit up in a mighty display of beautiful lights as the deck guns blasted, the missile defense satellites launched, laser batteries tracked incoming targets and fried them. The first salvo of a thousand homing missiles was only a few hundred meters out from the battleship when they detonated en masse. Not designed to damage, or to destroy the enemy systems, these missiles released millions of pieces of chaff into the vacuum of space. Chaff that confused the anti-missile systems.

"Shadow Squadron, pick your targets. You're free to engage," Germana said as he unleashed a devastating blast from his wing-mounted plasma canons at the closest pod in the battleship's missile defense system. It may have seemed like overkill, but it just added to the debris, and to the confusion.

"Shakedown, hit 'em and hit 'em hard, one pass. Then

I want you to double back, and do it again. We just launched another salvo," Commander Crom's voice came over the squadron channel.

"Roger that ,*Kentucky*. Any other birds make it off the ship?"

"Not yet. The ship's still under seige, but Reaper Squadron is preparing to launch," Crom said, proud. He'd been a member of Reaper before being promoted to commander.

"I thought they were pinned down," Shakedown said as he blasted the next pod.

"Drak marines relieved them. Those bastards are fierce in a fight," Crom said.

"You don't have to tell me."

The comms channel went quiet as the Spartan of Shadow Five, Rockstar, erupted in a bright flash, then was simply gone. Blasted into oblivion by one of the main deck's battle cannons. The rest of Shadow Squadron dove south, beneath the line of fire of the upper deck, and fired at the remaining anti-missile pods.

"AMDS destroyed. Three seconds to impact," Shadow Four, Burnout, called out.

And then the battleship was slammed by three-hundred-ninety antimatter warheads that made it through the missile defense. Its shields caved immediately as the first few struck. And then the rest found the battleship's hull, bees to the hive. The missile's outer casings smashed apart on impact, destroying the magnetic jars that held the warheads. Simple devices really. Without the powerful electromagnets shielding the antimatter from contact with regular matter the result was guaranteed. Matter-antimatter annihilation. A one-hundred percent conversion of matter to energy.

Shadow Squadron dove beneath the battleship's hull, and engaged their hyperdrives. Staying within system, but escaping the blast zone. When they emerged from hyperspace the enemy battleship was a burning wreck, listing heavily to port and slowing diving galactic south, it looked like an ocean vessel sinking. Moments later the sky lit up, white light blanketing the battlefield, as the hull cracked in half and the ship exploded.

Shakedown picked up six friendly fighters on his scanners. Reaper Squadron. *Too bad they were so late getting to the fight. They would have been useful a few minutes ago*, he thought. They formed up with Reaper and fell in behind the next wave of missiles. Not antimatter ordinance this time, simply conventional plutonium based fusion weapons. But it would be enough to deal with the remaining frigates, corvettes, and destroyers that survived Shadow Squadron's bombing run.

With the combined effect of another missile bombardment from the *Kentucky*, and Reaper and Shadow Squadrons hitting them hard, the enemy fleet crumbled. Only one ship made it away, jumping to hyperspace before the Spartans closed. It wasn't the only one that tired to flee, just the only one that succeeded. A human frigate. *Insignificant*, Shakedown thought.

"All Squadrons this is *Kentucky*. Great job Spartans, come on home!"

Reaper headed north of the ecliptic, banking hard over the wreckage of the enemy fleet to search for survivors. Too much interference from radiation to scan, so they searched visually. Shadow headed south, beneath the Kentucky, scanning the debris field of the Fifth Fleet.

"Sir, I'm picking up vital signs. There are survivors on the *Eisenhower*," Burnout called out over squad comms. "Fifteen, Sir."

"Kentucky, we're going to need search and rescue. There's survivors on the *Ike*, Repeat, survivors on the *Ike*."

A search and rescue team departed the *Kentucky* immediately, in a Northrop LS-5 Hercules shuttle.

Germana suspected that the dark fleet they'd faced was feeling sick of the Republic sending them into the meat grinder. That they'd betrayed the Republic because it no longer cared about them, its warriors. Shakedown knew many enlisted men who were disenfranchised, and many officers as well. It had only been a matter of time before they turned on the Republic. He'd felt it in his gut for years. He was wounded on Sullon III and nearly died, slaughtered dozens of curmians, and all for nothing. In the end the Republic recalled the Space Force from the system, withdrew its marines from the planet's surface, and rained devastation upon the world with a series of orbital bombardments. Thousands of Republicans died, and millions of curmian rebels. Lieutenant Germana knew that if circumstances had been a little different that it could have been him on the other side of the fight. He understood what it was like to be bitter at the Republic.

Shakedown and Burnout landed on the wreckage of the *Eisenhower's* hull after converting to mech mode. The forty-foot robots they piloted magnetically sealed their feet to the destroyed ship. The other seven members of Shadow Squadron patrolled the area, searching through the rest of the debris field that was once the Republic Fifth Fleet.

A few minutes later and there was laughing and rejoicing over the fleet channel as the shuttle team began the survivors' evac. Fifteen in total. The last remaining members of a crew of two thousand. Captain Harn among them.

When the final survivor boarded the shuttle and they began the flight back to the *Kentucky*, Shadow Ten —Pulsar — picked up enemy fighters emerging from hyperspace. "Twelve bandits inbound. One o'clock high," she called out.

In response the *Kentucky* acquired target lock and opened up on them with its deck cannons, and its missile batteries. Many of the cannons did not have line of sight, leaving the enemies obscured behind the fleet's debris. No missiles made it to impact, all shot down by the incoming fighters, but the deck cannons that managed to get a shot off fried one of the enemy fighters right off the bat. The black Spartan's shields were no match for the might of the carrier's heaviest cannons. It erupted in a fireball, spiraling out of formation and out of control, before exploding into so many jagged, glowing pieces of plasteel, tritanium, and ceramite growing ever colder in the vacuum.

"Shuttle crew, bring the survivors home immediately. Shadow Squadron, Reaper Squadron, engage these new fighters. No mercy," Commander Crom said over the fleet channel. "Kill every frakkin' one of those traitorous dogs! For the Fifth Fleet! For the Republic!"

18

"What do you mean the Fifth Fleet is MIA? Find a way to patch me through to Admiral Drex, now! I don't care if you have to send a holoprjection into his frakking toilet!" Chancellor Krell screamed at his chief of staff, Taric Lorn.

The bald, out-of-shape, middle-aged man stood trembling before Krell, who was a full head taller. They were alone in the chancellor's office on New Terra, an opulent room that garishly displayed Krell's personal wealth and influence of his station. A hundred artifacts lined the walls and filled display cabinets. Each one priceless beyond compare, and each from a civilization destroyed by the Republic, The day had been one of the most disastrous in the history of the Republic already, and Lorn feared that the chancellor was only going to make it worse.

"Sir, as you wish, of course…but, might I just…" Lorn was cut short as Krell backhanded him.

The chief of staff had never seen the chancellor react violently. Though he doubted it would be the last time he did. Lorn wiped blood from the corner of his mouth, "right away, Mr. Chancellor."

The chief of staff returned to the chancellor's office twenty minutes later. The sound of rebellion already brewing in the streets. From what holo footage he'd seen on the monitors it was already chaos, and spreading fast. If they didn't take serious precautions, Lorn knew they would be the first to burn when the Republic burst into the inferno that it inevitably would. Perhaps it was their destiny. But he had better plans than dying for the rotting husk of the Terran Republic.

"And?" Chancellor Krell asked as soon as Lorn was within earshot.

Lorn didn't answer until he had closed the distance between them. The office was as immense as it was luxurious, containing multiple libraries, relaxation areas, and even a kitchen. All were accessible off the main room, which was a long hallway. One that seemed too long as Lorn kept eye contact with the chancellor. Fifty, maybe sixty paces. *How much office does one man need?* Lorn wondered to himself, not for the first time.

When he got to the end of the crimson Valrusian rug Lorn cleared his throat, and leaned over the chancellor's desk, gripping the front with his hands until all the blood went from his knuckles. "Sir, the fleet is gone. The *last* fleet still loyal...is no more. I assume they fought valiantly, but STARCOM confirms..." Lorn felt the sting of Krell's backhand again, on the opposite cheek. A tooth flew from his mouth and landed on the marble floor, clattered across the recently buffed surface, and came to rest beneath a sculpture of some exotic green crystal, from some extinct race.

"Taric, you are as incompetent as any chief of staff who has ever served this Republic. STARCOM was compromised right from the start," Krell's disdain oozed from him in undulating waves of anger. A thick vein appeared on his forehead.

"Mr. Chancellor, I didn't…" Taric Lorn tried to plea. But it was too late. Krell had a pistol in hand, concealed beneath the heavy oak desk, when Lorn arrived. A single blast ended the chief of staff's ass kissing in mid-sentence.

Krell stood up, waited for his smoking blaster to cool, and wiped a smudge of carbon from the barrel with his cloak. Lorn fell forward onto the desk with a *thud*, missing half his face. The Valrusian rug absorbing brains and blood.

"What a mess. Any other day and I'd have the maintenance bots clean that carpet immediately," Jamin Krell said to himself. "But today isn't like any other day, is it?"

Krell knew that the Republic had died. That the thousand worlds were silent, and the people mostly yet unaware, mattered little. The fleets had all been destroyed. Fed to the Vargon, or smashed by the Coalition, it didn't matter. They were gone. And all that stood between Fleet Admiral Valdana and the chancellorship was time. If indeed the new order would even be a democratic system. Krell doubted it. He imagined Valdana in the diamond tiara of a ballet dancer from ancient Old Terra, the thought bringing him to laughter.

"He probably wants to be the frakkin' emperor of the

galaxy," Krell said out loud again. He'd learned in his forty-eight years as Chancellor to trust only himself. As a result he'd developed a habit of talking to himself. If his opponents had only known, they wouldn't have had to take military action. They could have crucified him on the cross of public opinion. A chancellor with a mental disorder hadn't served since before the Great War. And even then, the chancellor was removed from office, prompting the senate to pass the Mental Aptitude Act.

Krell hit a button on his desk and a holoprojector came to life, showing a Space Force pilot in exosuit. She removed her helmet to speak with the chancellor.

"Sir, we are prepared to launch. Lieutenant Bonn and the mechanic Royce are aboard. We await only your arrival," the pilot said.

"I'll be there in five minutes, Commander Krade. I have one stop to make before we depart. Before we leave the Republic to burn…"

"I don't think that is a good idea, Mr. Chancellor. Washington City is absolute chaos. We need to leave, and we need to leave now," the commander said.

"You are a Space Force commander. Get it together. I will be fine. We will launch as scheduled. I have my prae-torians, and for that matter Max will be with me as well. We will see you in the hangar bay, in five minutes. Now that is an order, Commander!" the chancellor closed the holoprojector, straightened his collar, and walked out of the office. He stopped near the door into the main building and retrieved a small crystal cube from one of the display cases on his way out.

Chancellor Krell knew that he only had moments

before his private estate, Monticello, was overrun by the mob. He didn't blame them, not after the way the galactic news networks had spun the story. They were reporting a galaxy-wide war breaking out with the Drakon Confederation and blaming his administration for initiating it; of course they claimed illegally, and without senate approval. There was no mention of anything to do with the missing systems, nor of the Vargon. And certainly no mention of the Coalition. The cover-up had been a conspiracy devised in his own office. Krell thought it ironic that he found himself in hot water based on misinformation his own office was spreading. But such was the way of the galaxy. Such was the way of the Republic. Though it was a bloated leviathan of treachery and red-tape, he still loved it.

Krell sprinted through the hallways of the sprawling complex, pushing aside the thought of taking a moment to look upon some of his more exotic, priceless works of art one last time. He got to the west wing, where the bedchambers were, dashing up the winding, carpeted staircase to the second floor. He switched on the comms system on his left wrist as he continued to run down the hallway, toward her room.

"Praetors, you are to disengage the mobs and fall back into the mansion. Regroup at the level four hangar. Commander Krade is waiting to depart in four minutes. Anyone who doesn't make it will be left behind," Krell spoke into his wrist-mic, focusing on not panting.

He switched from his security channel to a private one. A channel which he shared with only one other person, Max. His android wife. The synthoid who so many scandals centered upon, around, or near. Their marriage had been a walking political catastrophe, but that just made him love her more.

"Max, we're leaving sweetheart. Now! Are you packed, dear?" Krell said just as he got to the giant maple double doors to his bedchamber. He only heard the sound of the shower. They were under attack and had to run for their very lives, flee the capital, flee New Terra altogether, and she was in the frakking shower.

He pushed the doors open, feeling the thick grooves in the grains of the wood that had worn into them over the millennia since they'd been used in a temple on Old Terra for the last time. Krell marveled at how smooth the chips, dents, and notches had become over time. Each one telling him a thousand stories, of galactic conquest, or empires that rose and fell across the stars long before he was born. It sickened him to have to leave it all behind.

Jamin Krell ran into the bathroom of the master suite, kicked the door open, and yelled, "come on, Max! Now! There is an angry mob at the gates that wants to see us dead!"

"Don't be so dramatic, sweetheart. When isn't there an angry mob..." the android said, as she rinsed shampoo out of her hair.

"You know I hate rhetorical questions. We need to leave, NOW!" he screamed, his face flush. A thick vein stuck out on Krell's forehead. "They are going to kill us, dear! We are going to die, if we don't leave right frakkin' now!"

"Okay, okay. I just need to get dressed, and pack a few things. I'll need to take shoes, and clothes I assume. How long do you think we will be gone, baby?" the naiveté poured from her perfect synthoid mouth.

"Throw on a towel, if you take any more time than that then we will probably die. I told the praetors to go on to the ship," Krell said, more frustrated than he'd ever been in his life. Ironically it was moments just like that which made Krell feel most attracted to Max. She could frustrate him more than any flesh and blood woman in the galaxy, and nothing got him hot under the collar like frustration.

"And why would you go and do such a thing, silly?" she teased, winking at him.

Max stepped from the shower, a dripping wet image of feminine perfection. The most perfect woman that Sony Galactic Industries had ever produced, according to their own claims. And who would know better how to make a perfect sex-robot than the only corporation who had been building them since before mankind first departed from Old Terra out into the darkness. She put on a towel, wrapped another one around her hair and offered her hand, daintily, to her husband.

"Don't worry doll, there's plenty of clothing on board the ship," Krell comforted his wife as they rushed down the hallway.

"Oh, I'm getting the Valrusian rugs all wet," Max cried out.

"Max, the odds are we are never coming back. And if we do, there likely won't be a rug left to worry about," Krell snapped at her. "What part of *fleeing into exile* don't you get, my love?"

They got back to the first floor and made it to the

elevator just as the first sounds of blaster fire cut through the air. Krell opened his security comm channel.

"Praetors, the first lady and myself are en route to the hangar. We are in the elevator off the main concourse. Any of you not aboard *Space Force One* are advised to evac by whatever means available. There are shuttles on deck five, though I am unsure how many," Krell said. He knew that many fine soldiers had probably already died to protect him that day, and he would never get to thank them for their sacrifice. He got choked up thinking about it.

"Darling, they are soldiers. This is their duty, to protect you," she spoke in her Old Terran Eastern European accent. The one she used when she wasn't trying to be subtle in her attempts to manipulate him. In this case though, he knew she was right.

"To those who continue to fight for the safety and security of the first family, you have my undying gratitude, as well as the gratitude of the Terran Republic," Krell addressed his security force again as the lift doors opened up to the hangar. Two praetorians were coming out of the adjacent lift. One saw Krell and Max and got his partner's attention as he gave the chancellor a thumbs up.

The two praetorians rushed across the hangar, their hulking power armored frames shielded the chancellor and the first lady as best they could. The four moved together across hangar and up the ramp to *Space Force One*. As soon as the chancellor was aboard blaster fire turned the air into a hot steaming display of brilliant flashes around them. The praetorians and the boarding ramp were bombarded with dozens of blasts before they could retaliate. Krell knew by the sound of it a heavy blaster was the weapon being used against them. Probably an MG-57.

The first praetor advanced back down the ramp, toward the closest enemy, launching wrist mounted proton rockets at targets he'd yet to see but were picked out by his targeting AI systems. The second guardsman huddled his large form over the tiny android Max, guiding her to safety inside the ship.

"Good thing we saw you praetors," Krell said. "You just saved our lives."

"Just doing my duty, Sir," the crimson armored guardsman said as he turned to head back down the ramp.

"Wait, praetor?" Krell realized he'd never bothered to learn the man's name.

"Ginn. Praetor G-247, or just Ginn, Sir," the guardsman said.

"We need every man we can get. Stay on this ship, that's an order," Krell said, turning toward the cockpit. "Commander Krade, light these fools up as soon as the last guardsman is clear!"

But it was too late. A swarm of lower-level scum from the inner hives had filled the hangar. Despite the praetor's superior weaponry and armor he was surrounded by a hoard, a rock in an ocean. An ocean which broke around him and was heading toward the ship.

The praetor's plasma cannons overheated, so he pulled his side arm. A wicked, fifty cal slug thrower, made by Lockheed specially for the praetorian guard, which fired explosive or incendiary rounds. He turned his back on the approaching horde knowing it would take the combined strength of dozens to topple him in his power armor with his mag-boots sealed as they were. He was planted like a tralgin tree on a high gravity world. The praetor began to unload on the rioters closest to the ship. Krell watched over the monitors as several heads and torsos exploded, shattered by the explosive rounds. Though the crimson armored cyborg's voracious attacks did little to stem the flow of the tide.

And then a rocket propelled grenade was fired from behind the praetor, from the cover of a palette of cargo crates. The attacker with the shoulder mounted rocket launcher appeared on the holoscreen for the briefest of moments before ducking back behind cover, as Krell watched helplessly from within the ship. There was nothing he could do but watch as the grenade tore through half a dozen rioters after smashing the praetor in the back. The explosion rocked the entire hangar, leaving nothing of the praetor but two crimson power armored legs, mag-sealed to the ground.

The remaining praetor went to the ramp and unloaded on the screaming mob with a customized M-85. As he did so his targeting systems locked on to the most likely spot from which the grenade had fired. He unleashed the rest of his shoulder-mounted rockets in a single salvo, destroying the far side of the hangar entirely. The roof started to cave in.

"Get that ramp up, and get us out of here, Commander!" Krell yelled down the cabin toward the cockpit.

Space Force One's repulsors lifted the ship up as the ion engines hummed to life. It rotated ninety degrees, and oriented toward the hangar doors. Then, just as the ceiling collapsed, crushing many rioters flat and wounding many others with falling debris, Commander Krade launched at reckless speeds from the hangar. They rocketed out of danger as the rest of the hangar collapsed. The few surviving rioters fired small arms at the ship, but missed horribly as Krade took evasive maneuvers.

Monticello was situated on a cliff, above a three-hundred meter waterfall adjacent the hangars. Every shuttle and ship that came and went from the estate was treated to one of the most breathtaking views in the known galaxy. It was the envy of many a noble, on many a world. And Krell sighed deeply at the thought of never seeing it again. The fact that they'd flown by it at incredible speeds, leaving them unable to enjoy the view one last time, cut Chancellor Jamin Krell to his core.

"Sir," Commander Krade's voice came over the holo-screen as her image projected from a table in front of Krell. "I just received word that a dozen praetorians made it to a ship and are falling into formation behind us. What system are we jumping to? I need to send the coordinates to their navicomputer."

"The Thurian system, Commander. If we're going to rebuild the Republic, we're going to need a fleet," the chancellor said. "Now, where is agent Royce? Is she not aboard?"

19

The *Banshee's Lament* emerged from hyperspace and into a field of debris. Random remains of the Republic Fifth Fleet smashed into the ship every few seconds as Krynn and Lemmy took evasive action.

"Full power to forward shields, Lem," Felo Krynn called out as he barrel rolled past the remains of one of a battleship's quad cannons. "Open a channel to the *Kentucky*, and whatever else may be left of the fleet."

This ship rocked as the remains of a Spartan smashed into its hull. Krynn saw the dogfight between Republican Spartans and their Coalition counterparts with his eyes before his scanning systems alerted him to the situation. Brilliant flashes of white, red, and yellow filled the battle zone.

Lemmy growled something under his breath as the ship's computer alerted Krynn that the *Kentucky* required they provide Republic authorization codes before it saw them as a friendly, and that failing to do so, they would be blown out of the sky.

"Miller!" Krynn yelled across the ship. "Get up here, now! They aren't accepting my ID codes and think we are an enemy vessel. We just jumped into a shitstorm."

"I got this, Krynn," Miller said with no sense of urgency in her voice.

Miller put her helmet on, opened her squadron channel, and spoke to her Spartans. "Shadow Squadron, this is Valkyrie. Shadow Squadron, this is Valkyrie. I am aboard the *Banshee's Lament*. Do you copy?"

"Whoo-hoo!"

"Glad to hear from you, Captain! We heard you were dead!" Shakedown's voice came through the crackling static.

"Tell the *Kentucky* to stand down! We are having trouble with our ID authentication, and they are about to blow us out of the sky!" Miller said as she found her sense of urgency.

Krynn was busy taking evasive maneuvers to avoid incoming fire from the *Kentucky*. They were more or less warning shots. Small yield devices. If they impacted they wouldn't be enough to destroy the ship outright, but it would certainly be crippled, possibly dead in the water.

"*Kentucky*, Shakedown. Stand down. The light cruiser is with us. Captain Miller is aboard! Valkyrie is aboard the cruiser," the Spartan pilot exclaimed, joy and excitement in his tone.

"Shakedown, *Kentucky* actual. Roger that!" Admiral Drex's voice replied. The Spartans heard cheering throughout the CIC as the crew celebrated Miller's return.

"Shakedown, can you patch us through to the *Kentucky*? Somehow these Coalition fighters are jamming our comms," Miller said, again over the squadron channel. She wondered about Krynn's boasts of having the best tech and how much validity there was to them.

"Can do, Sir!" Shakedown replied as the *Lament* fell into formation with Shadow Squadron, who was regrouping as Lieutenant Colt and Reaper Squadron initiated an attack run.

"Krynn, we're on fleet comms now. Patch through my squadron's channel," Miller yelled across the ship.

"Good! Now, mount the quad cannons! We need every bit of help we can get," Krynn sounded concerned. "These guys are using tech like I've never seen…and I thought I'd seen it all. They are teleporting through mobile, single-fighter worm-holes."

Miller ran across the ship, and climbed the ladder to the quad cannon. It was an old model, out of date even before the Great War broke out, but it was the kind of weapon that really packed a punch. Miller laughed as she got into the cannon's chair, separated from the vacuum of space by a simple looking clear dome.

"What the frak is this, Krynn?" Miller chided. "I didn't know you were an antique collector."

"I thought you saw it when you were on top of the hull, back on Lyra," Krynn laughed. "Glad I exceeded your expectations."

"I was too busy being shot at by an angry mob back on Lyra," Miller said as she unleashed a series of blasts from the cannons at a passing enemy fighter that had fallen out of formation with its squadron. "And by the way, that boarding ramp works just fine, Krynn."

Felo Krynn simply laughed at her remarks. He'd

wondered how long it was going to take her to bring it up. "Looks like I owe you five credits, Lemmy."

A moment later and all bandits were gone. Simply invisible to all scanning frequencies. "Are they stealth?" Burnout asked the squadron. "I didn't detect any hyper-space signature."

"No. They're gone, for now. It's how the Coalition has been attacking. They warp in, through wormholes. They hit, they leave, without a trace. Not even a hyperspace signature," Krynn said.

"The Coalition?" Shakedown asked. "Is that what these traitors call themselves?"

"Yeah," Miller said. "They destroyed the fleets. They destroyed the Republic today, in all but name. And even that probably won't take too long."

"Damn," Burnout and Shakedown said simultaneously.

"They destroyed the frakkin' Confederation's fleets as well," Miller continued. "The Coalition is who attacked us at Lyra. The drak part of their fleet at least."

The emptiness of space shimmered as a wormhole opened, as wide as a battleship, right in the flight path of Reaper Squadron. The Spartans scrambled and broke off in every direction. Some diving, some climbing, some peeling off at incredible speeds. If it weren't for the iner-tial dampening systems and the exosuits the pilots wore the G's would have turned them into splattered goo in their cockpits.

The wormhole slammed closed nearly as fast as it had appeared, disgorging dozens of plasma mines like vomit from the mouth of a sick predator. The more the squadron tried to evade them the more wormholes opened in their zone, each spilling forth more mines. In moments all of Reaper Squadron was surrounded by a minefield. A minefield that was growing exponentially, with increasing rapidity.

Despite the pilots of Space Force having the fastest reflexes of any members of the Republican military Reaper Four was unable to avoid colliding with one of the plasma mines when a wormhole dumped it right on top of him. If he'd had ten more milliseconds he might have made it, just the tip of his wing clipped the magnetized shell of the mine. But that was all it took. Just the tip.

A chain reaction was set off. In a flash the entire mine field ignited in a blinding ball of plasma that for a moment obscured the battle zone. There were no screams, no cries for help. No wounded soldier alerts over the fleet comms. There were no shattered Spartans in pieces, littering the battle zone with hot metal. No bodies to recover. There was nothing left of Reaper Squadron but a hot cloud of vapor. Krynn's scanners showed the squadron was nearly entirely atomized by the plasma storm the mines unleashed.

"All ships, return to *Kentucky*. All ships, RTB immediately," Commander Crom's voice filled Miller's ears as she choked back her instinct to scream.

Shadow Squadron was completely silent. They fell into formation and headed for the carrier without even a cough, or heavy breathing. The *Lament*, still in tight formation with the squadron, seemed an appropriate ship to accompany them in that moment. *Appropriate at least in name*, Miller thought.

ALEISTER DAVIDSON

The squadron landed in the main hangar as it always did, the *Banshee's Lament* along with the rest of the ships. Before Miller and Krynn had disembarked an emergency alert came up on the cockpit's holoscreen. An alert from the OCR.

"Miller, get in here," Felo Krynn called out to her, unaware of her location in the ship. He figured after Reaper Squadron was annihilated that she was tied up in knots inside. "There's an incoming message from the chancellor's office."

"Be right there, Krynn," Miller replied. She sounded like she'd been punched in the gut. Deflated, as if the joy of life had gone out of her.

Miller got to the cockpit and took the copilot's chair. Lemmy let her sit up front so that she could see the holoscreen.

"This is Krynn," the captain answered the call. "What can I do for you?"

"Hold for the Chancellor of the Republic," the sultry voice of his nemesis, Commander Krade came over the dash-mounted speakers.

A solid five minutes went by with nothing but static on the line. Then the baritone voice of Chancellor Jamin Krell came over the speakers and a blue-green hologram of his face was cast above the control panels.

"Captain Krynn, I am en route to the Thurian system as we speak," the chancellor said. "I am in exile, having barely escaped New Terra with my life. The Coalition is in power now, throughout the galaxy. The Drako fleets that remain loyal to the Confederation are embroiled in bitter conflict over the future of their race. But us...the fleets

156

that remain have sided with the Coalition, under Fleet Admiral Valdana."

"We have a plan, Mr. Chancellor." Krynn said, exuding confidence. "We boarded the *Kentucky*, but were just under attack by Coalition forces using tech like I've never seen before. Wormhole tech. They dropped a mine-field on us through thousands of wormholes. Reaper Squadron was destroyed outright, completely vaporized."

"That is grave news indeed, Captain. Inform Admiral Drex that I will be arriving soon. We are less than thirty minutes out," the chancellor said. "Oh, and one last thing. I hope it doesn't become a problem, but Agent Royce is aboard *Space Force One* with us."

"And why would that be a problem, Sir?"

"I know you two were married. The operative word being were," the chancellor laughed as he spoke. "If it were any of my ex-wives…Well, let's just say I wouldn't be too happy to see them."

"We are both Void Ops agents, Sir. The best of the best in the galaxy."

"You still haven't answered my question, Captain."

"You have my word, Mr. Chancellor. The mission comes first, no matter what."

"Admiral, I have returned from Lyra. I am bringing a new contact, Captain Krynn to meet with you. He has urgent news from the Chancellor of the Republic. My mission has been successful," Miller spoke into her helmet as they travelled up the lift to the bridge. She knew that Krynn couldn't hear her, but somehow he still shot her a reassuring glance. She wondered if KV-1N had the ability to listen in on encrypted military channels and was somehow passing her conversations on to Krynn. So far, Void Ops tech had been as advanced as anything she'd ever seen; short of the Vargon's.

The lift doors opened and Miller saw the all-too-familiar sign painted on the opposite wall of the corridor, though it was splattered with blood and gore. There were bodies and parts of bodies throughout the corridor. Medi-bots and crews worked to take them away. The cleaning bots had not yet gotten to the stain removal phase and Miller could tell that many more had died than the dozens of remaining bodies would indicate.

Miller took her helmet off, savoring the smell of the ship. Something she'd taken for granted too many times. Though she had to fight to find it beneath the coppery taste of blood in the air, the smell of home mixed well in her mind with the smell of death.

They headed left out of the lift, towards the admiral's quarters. Krynn followed behind Miller. Kevin issued a series of concerned sounding beeps. Krynn shrugged.

"I don't know. Maybe the Admiral is not on the bridge. I would assume he'd be in the CIC, but we didn't go there either, so who knows?" the roguish agent replied. "Nothing has been normal lately."

They got to the admiral's quarters and the door *whooshed* open before Miller could ring. The lighting in the room, a dull greenish glow, seemed oddly alien to Miller. It was not the usual full-spectrum bio-phosphorescent LED lighting she was used to in the admiral's quarters. She noted that the room stank of sulphur as she entered.

"Captain, it is good to see you. We have much to discuss. This is Commander Slaath," the admiral stood and gestured toward the reptoid cyborg.

Slaath stood and took Miller's hand in a firm grip and shook it profusely. He looked her deep in the eye and said, "Captain Miller, you have my undying gratitude. If it were not for your courage then I myself would not be here."

"If it weren't for Lieutenant Tova. She was my wing man. We both owe her our gratitude..." Miller said, her cheek quivering. "This is Captain Krynn, and the bot KV-1N. They have critical intel, as well as a message directly from the Chancellor of the Republic."

"Is that so?" Admiral Drex said, dismissively. "I know

who you are, Krynn. And so should you, Captain Miller. This man is a pirate, a smuggler, an assassin, a thief, and a tax evader. I know the list of charges goes on, but that's all I can remember off the top of my head. Now, this is what you bring me in this moment? Whatever he's got, it better be worth my time, Captain. Because anything short of that, and he gets put out the airlock...along with that fancy bot."

"Sir," Krynn saluted Drex. His whole demeanor changing in an instant. The slimy dirtbag replaced by a man of seriousness. A sense of valiance emanated from him as he stood at attention. "Assistant Deputy Director Felo Krynn, Republic Ministry of Intelligence Directorate of Operations, at your service, Admiral."

Drex took a deep breath, looked Krynn up and down like a space marine drill sergeant inspecting a new recruit, and turned his back. He walked a few feet over to his sideboard and poured four glasses of bourbon from a red glass decanter. He handed the first to Krynn, the second to Miller, and the third to Slaath, before lifting his own glass high.

"I'll drink to that!" Drex laughed. Then he saluted Krynn. "I'm a frakkin' admiral and I would have never known. Void Ops...huh." Drex shook his head in disbelief.

"Sir, the Chancellor will be arriving in system aboard *Space Force One* within minutes. New Terra has fallen, Washington City overrun by mobs of rioters. Monticello is now in the hands of rebels," Krynn said, a twinge of sadness his voice. A dimple in his chiseled jaw quivered for a moment before he continued. "The Coalition has all but destroyed Space Force. The *Kentucky* is now the last carrier. The few remaining ships that are still loyalists will be joining us. Any vessels aboard that are battle capable need to be brought online."

"So, the Coalition…that's what they call themselves. Traitorous dogs. Who leads these bastards?" Drex asked, though he knew the answer. Deep in his gut he knew that Krynn would say…

"Fleet Admiral Valdana," Krynn said. By the look on Drex's face he knew the admiral was not surprised. "He is in command of the Coalition. We know little about how they are structuring command, or how the humans and the draks are sharing power. But we do know there is already discontent spreading throughout their fleets.

The Confederation has put up a better fight than the Republic, but they have been unresponsive to our attempts to forge an alliance."

"We have a neural scan of the drak I followed to the Lyran moon, though Lieutenant Commander Blick was taken by the Coalition. Hopefully there is something of use in the drak's brain scans," Miller chimed in.

"How did you have time for that?" Slaath asked. "It would take weeks to develop a working model of a complex brain, even with the best facilities in the galaxy."

"Neutrino quantum mapping. Old tech from a long dead culture," Krynn said, dismissively, as if everyone had such a device. "Kevin, give us a look at the drak's memories."

The bot spun in place as it hovered, seemingly annoyed. It did its usual series of lights and beeps and then a blue beam emanated from its holoprojector. A blurry cloud became ever sharper and soon they were seeing through the eyes of the dead drakon marine. The bot fast-forwarded the projection searching for something of interest.

"Wait!" Slaath exclaimed at the bot, nearly jumping from his seat. The drak was not used to bourbon, and he was obviously enjoying its effects. "Go back a few frames. I saw someone I know."

KV-1N rewound the hologram until Slaath said, "there. right there."

Kevin started the playback again and Slaath was shocked. He stood up, gripped the table's edge until his claws bit into it, and began growling. A low pitched, guttural sound that rumbled unnaturally in his throat and resounded off his metallic lower jaw.

The humans let Slaath have his emotional space and did not acknowledge his anger. They watched intently as Fenn met with a drakon lieutenant in a cantina. It was not unlike the cantina in Mon Tarley. Some dingy frak of a dive bar full of scoundrels and miscreants.

Fenn produced a tablet, and pulled up a star map. With a flick of his finger the lieutenant sent coordinates from his own device to that of Fenn's. They shook hands, then the lieutenant stood up and walked out of the cantina.

"Vorn!" Slaath snarled, frothing at the mouth.

Admiral Fritz Yonk awoke to a throbbing head and whirling chaos around him. Smoke filled the CIC from several small electrical fires. The overwhelming smell of ozone was a welcome sensation to the admiral, as it reminded him he was still alive. It took him a full minute to realize that his plan to escape the shell that encompassed Gylian Secunda was a success. The *Vindicator* had made it out of the shell, though Yonk was sure that the fleet in orbit was lost.

When the admiral was given word that Lieutenant Bonn had used a shuttle to jump out of the system from the planet's atmosphere he initiated his own plan of escape. While Bonn had slipped between two of the hexagonal plates that ultimately formed the shell structure that surrounded the planet, that option was unavailable to the *Vindicator*. The Mars Class Lockheed B-209C Battleship was much too large to squeeze through, so the admiral had ordered the ship to ram.

He never thought it would work. With every ship on

both sides of the fight firing upon the plates and accomplishing nothing there had seemed little hope. But hope had seen the admiral and his crew through. With all power to forward shields, and every battery on the ship targeting the point of impact, the *Vindicator* rammed the closing sphere. It took everything the engines had to push through, and every bit of auxiliary power the ship could spare to keep the shields intact.

The collision was a spectacular event, sending resounding impact waves through the entire length of the battleship. The hull bulked and heaved, every surface quaked and quivered from the impact. The admiral was sure that the bow was destroyed. But somehow, as if guided by the hand of Jeru himself, the ship made it through.

When the admiral was able to get to his feet he watched the playback on the holoscreens of the events of their escape. When the Vindicator hit the plate it was an irresistible force hitting an immovable object. But the strange alien technology had simply absorbed the shock of the impact and spun in place like a coin on a table. It rotated upon an axis that seemed to be composed of the arcing plasma that connected the plates at their points. When the Vindicator hit, it struck at the corner, where two plates connected. The plasma connections glitched out for a moment, the plate spun in place as they'd passed through, and in moments had resumed its regular position.

Admiral Yonk had never seen the like. Then again he'd never seen Spacemen of the Republic side with draks and fight their own kind. It was impossible to tell what had survived of the fleet from what scans were showing. The impact was causing roving blackouts in electrical systems, though initial estimates were optimistic that there were at least a few survivors of the Republic Eighth Fleet.

Admiral Yonk dusted himself off, took note that several of his crewmen were incapacitated, some possibly dead, and made a mental note of what stations were unmanned. Thankfully his chief communications officer, Ensign Harek, was still at his post.

"Ensign Harek, open the fleet channel. I want a head count," the admiral ordered. "Have all remaining ships report in. We need to know what's left of the fleet."

A few minutes passed and the ensign reported that other than the *Vindicator* only one battlecruiser, one frigate, one corvette, and two destroyers remained of the fleet. The carrier *Iowa* was lost, as were its F-138 squadrons. The battlecruiser *Valiant*, Two destroyers, three frigates, and three corvettes were also destroyed within the planet eating sphere. The eighth fleet was still in the fight, though at a significantly reduced strength.

"Admiral, I am receiving a signal over the fleet channel. I haven't authenticated the ID codes yet, but it appears to be Chancellor Krell. It is a subspace communication, originating from hyperspace, but it is a priority one signal," Ensign Harek announced. He diligently returned to trying to authenticate the codes.

"Let me know as soon as the ID checks out. I'll take Krell's message in my quarters," Yonk said as he walked out of the ship's CIC and onto the lift.

The doors closed and Fritz Yonk fought back the sorrow that threatened to overwhelm him. Tens of thousands of his crewmen...dead. The entire planet of Gylian Secunda...gone. Vaporized. Atomized and sucked away through a wormhole. The weight of such loss hit him much harder than he was used to. There was nothing that he could do, he knew that. Admiral Yonk had lost thousands under his command over the years. But never so many at once. Never so many so quick. And never so many ships.

Yonk wondered if his heart had turned black, gone rotten. Part of him felt more keenly the loss of the ships than the loss of their crews. The part of him that was a realist, an admiral, and a Republican. But the rest of him hated that part, judged him as heartless, indifferent, and cruel. Yonk gave himself a sharp slap across the face. "Get your shit together, Admiral," he said to himself aloud as the lift reached its destination, deck seventeen.

He used every ounce of resilience and resolve he could muster to push down the feelings of loss pulling at his heart strings. Yonk knew there would be time to grieve, but it would be a long fight before that day came. He had a mission to do, and a Republic to save. The ships were important. He had to remind himself of that.

Admiral Yonk entered his quarters, walked to his bathroom, opened the medicine cabinet, and popped several pills. He knew that he needed to suppress his feelings, and that mood enhancers and battle stimms would put him in the headspace he needed to be in to lead the fleet. Yonk hated taking mood stabilizers and emotion suppressors. But he knew that he'd crossed a line when he felt survivor's guilt over being happy so many ships survived. The rational part of his mind told him it was alright to rejoice at still having nearly half the fleet intact. But the part of him that was shattered at the loss of so many under his command hated that part of him. And the fleet would suffer if he was being torn apart inside by cognitive dissonance.

A few minutes later and the pills kicked in. And Admiral Yonk again felt normal. Too normal. That was the only way he could describe the sensation. Or lack thereof. His mind was as clear as it had ever been, but his heart was shut off entirely. Emotionally, the admiral was numb. He wondered why it was that Space Force regulations didn't require officers to stay in such a state at all times. *Surely it is most optimal*, he thought.

A chirping sound came from the computer in his cabin. The signal that Ensign Harek was finished with the code authentication. "Put him through," the admiral said to the AI.

"Admiral," Harek cleared his throat. "The code checks out. It is from the chancellor's office. It originated from *Space Force One*, and was sent via tech I really don't know how to explain. It looks like it was sent to realspace from hyperspace, but through nonconventional means. Possibly a wormhole, and probably alien tech."

"I've had it up to my neck with wormholes. Have engineering look into it, but the chancellor has a lot of tech at his disposal that we *plebs* do not," the admiral said before breaking out into a mirthless laugh. "Patch the message through to my holoprojector."

Fritz Yonk poured himself a vodka, kicked his feet up on his table, and turned on the holoprojector.

"Admiral Yonk, we are condition Omega. The

Republic has fallen. The Coalition now reigns throughout the galaxy," the chancellor's hologram spoke. "We are piecing together a loyalist fleet from whatever ships remain. Your orders are to rendezvous with the remaining Republican forces in the Thurian system immediately."

The holofeed ended and the chancellor faded away. The cabin seemed empty and lifeless without the hologram speaking. Yonk poured himself another vodka, this time with soda and a twist of lime. He slammed the glass down in one large gulp, spilling much of his drink on his collar.

Admiral Yonk put on his beret and patched his holofeed into every monitor and projector in the fleet. "Men and women of the Third Fleet. The Republic has fallen. I just heard it straight from the chancellor himself. We are called into action, now, on behalf of that lost Republic. The Coalition now rules from New Terra, and throughout the galaxy. And it is up to us, the survivors of this terrible day, to put an end to their reign. To restore the Republic. All captains, set course for the Thurian system. We are joining what remains of loyal Republican fleets. The odds are against us. But our cause is righteous. Whatever it was that we faced in the Gylian system must be dealt with. But we cannot face those insurmountable odds until we have taken out our trash. Until we have purged the cancer that is this traitorous Coalition from our dear Republic!"

Cheers went up throughout all the fleet, crescendoing into a deafening roar over Yonk's speaker system. An alien threat destroying planets was one thing; the kind of thing which Space Force was intended to deal with. But the

Republic being destroyed from the inside out by traitors...
men and women he'd fought beside...it made Fritz Yonk
sick to his stomach. For Republicans to betray everything
they'd ever stood for was unforgivable as far as he was
concerned. And Yonk saw red, thirsting for the blood of
every traitor. In his gut he knew that Fleet Admiral
Valdana was behind it all. No other officer had been so
outspoken a critic of Chancellor Krell as Valdana...the
only five star flag officer currently serving in the Space
Force. *It would explain why so many joined his cause*, Yonk
thought. *He's the senior commander of the Space Force.*

"Today we jump into the lungs of hell itself," Yonk
continued when the crews quieted. "This is it. The last
stand of the Terran Republic. This is our worst nightmare. This is mankind's darkest hour, and I would not face
it with any others. I am proud to lead you fine Spacemen
into battle once again. I would have it no other way.

"All ships, prepare to make the jump to Thuria on my
mark. For liberty! For freedom! For the Republic!"

P rivate Gorn got a notification on his HUD. The two marines who had stayed behind in the hangar with the shuttle were dead. A moment later Commander Slaath's voice crackled over the squad channel.

"Men, Lieutenant Vorn is a traitor. He revealed our position to the Coalition. It appears that he has murdered the marines who remained with the shuttle. Ensign Grix is still showing on scanners as alive, though he does appear to be wounded. Men, I need you to get back down to the shuttle, and kill Vorn before he can cause any more mischief," Commander Slaath issued his orders in an unfamiliar, sober tone.

"Roger that, Commander," Gorn answered, though he was not in charge. "We'll make that bastard pay."

Corporal Tegg was now officially in command of the marines. Followed by Private First Class Brinn. Gorn had spoken out of turn when dealing with the Commander, and Tegg was glowering at him. Hurd and Vallek chuckled lightly to themselves. None of them ever thought Snett would buy the farm. He was the hardest marine any of them had ever seen. Tough as tritanium nails. Tegg had never mentally prepared to command the squad, but he'd always told himself he was ready. Just lies to keep the voice in the back of his head quiet. The voice that said, *"don't worry about it. Nothing's ever gonna happen to Sarge."*

Except it had. Snett had died to save his men. And now Tegg had to step up and lead them in not just a mission, but an act of revenge. There was a grim determination that gripped them all, a heaviness of the soul that weighed upon their chests and made it harder to breath than it should have been. Lieutenant Vorn was Snett's right hand. They'd flown from one side of the galaxy to the other with him. But none of them had ever liked him. He was odd, uncomfortable. Even for a drakon. A sour grape in an otherwise sweet bunch. Vorn was always the odd man out, and Major Bast's nemesis on the *Infernal*.

The five marines hit the lift in silence. Tegg punched the button to take them down to the lower decks. The hangar was one long, straight shot to the shuttle. There were machines, equipment, and vehicles throughout that would make good cover. But there would be no hiding the fact that they were coming from Vorn.

Private Gorn's heart leapt up into his throat as the lift doors opened. He switched his view to infrared, and with the Confederation ID tags, was able to confirm that Vorn and Grix were still aboard the shuttle.

"Men, this is a hostage situation. I'm opening a channel to the shuttle. I want to talk to the lieutenant," Corporal Tegg said. Gorn wasn't sure that Tegg was full of confidence, and it wasn't the play he himself would have called, but he didn't dare question the Corporal. They needed to act with one mind, with total cohesion.

Tegg flipped up a panel on his armor's left forearm. He keyed a few buttons and was patched into the shuttle's channel.

"Vorn, let the ensign go. We can talk about this," Tegg said.

Nothing. Only silence.

"Lieutenant Vorn. I know you are there. You are to let Ensign Grix go immediately. There's no way out of this for you, Lieutenant. But you let Grix go...I'll personally make sure you get treated fairly," the Corporal lied.

"Treated fairly? I'll be seen as a traitor. No, I'd rather not let Grix go. He's all I've got," Vorn finally answered. "But make no mistake. Any attempt to storm the shuttle and I will shoot him."

"Roger that," Tegg replied as he gestured for his men to move forward.

The marines moved from cover to cover though they had a perfect view of Vorn with their helmets' infrared abilities. The heat signature of Ensign Grix was slowly fading. It wouldn't be long until he died.

"I don't think he's gonna make it anyway, Corporal," Gorn said. "Let's blow this frakkin' ship and call it done."

"We can't give up on him, Private. He's a Confederation Navy officer," Tegg replied. "Now move!"

The marines approached the ship after Private Hurd threw an EMP grenade under the rear starboard landing strut. The ship's electronics were fried long enough for them to make it to the loading ramp undetected. Tegg was the first one through the ship's rear door, followed by Gorn and Brinn. Vallek and Hurd came through last.

The ship was open. Gorn thought that it was odd that the Lieutenant didn't bother to at least bring the loading ramp up.

"I've got a bad feeling about this, Corporal," Gorn said. "He wouldn't just let us walk in here unless it was a frakkin' trap."

"Noted. Men, disembark from this shuttle. We'll figure out another way to do this," Tegg ordered.

Vallek, Hurd, and Brinn were back out in the hangar when they heard the sound of blaster fire. The squad watched in unison through the infrared as Grix was shot through the head. His body fell forward and grew ever colder in their HUDs.

"Take him!" Tegg ordered.

Private Gorn went through the ship first, followed closely by Tegg. The other three marines shrugged, exchanged glances, and hustled back up the ramp onto the ship.

Gorn made it into the shuttle's cockpit first. It was larger than that of most shuttles in its class, and Vorn stood over the body of Grix with his blaster still smoking at the far end. Grix lay in the aisle, Vorn stood between the pilot's and copilot's seats, laughing.

Private Gorn had his weapon leveled, ready to put a round right through Lieutenant Vorn's eye. Tegg entered behind him.

"Put your weapon down, Lieutenant," Gorn said. No emotion in his voice.

"You are too late. Fools," Vorn said as he touched a

small box on his belt. Neither marine had noticed it before the Lieutenant hit a button on it. It appeared ordinary, like an ammo pouch, or some utility device. But it caused space-time to tear itself apart around Vorn. Gorn and Tegg fired into the spot where he stood, a moment too late...watching in disbelief as Vorn disappeared through a wormhole. In an instant he was gone.

Gorn opened his mouth to speak but no words came. He was vaporized as the shuttle exploded in a white-hot fireball.

"All decks, report!" Admiral Vallon Drex's voice resounded throughout the ship over the klaxons. Drex had never felt such an enormous explosion hit the *Kentucky*, let alone come from within its bowels. From the way the ship rocked Drex was fairly certain that a tactical nuclear device had gone off in the hangar.

The thought troubled him to his core. He knew that Slaath's shuttle had been scanned for weapons on the way into the hangar. He also knew that there had been no such device aboard the Confederation ship. Which meant only one thing. The Coalition had used the same technology as they had with their boarding parties; except a tactical nuclear device had come through the wormhole. Drex clenched his jaw tight at the realization that he should've seen it coming.

The next half-hour was filled with damage reports and repair protocols being initiated. Drex felt as if he'd talked to every single officer on the *Kentucky* by the time he was done. The ship had a half-kilometer long hole in the hull.

Several hangars across several decks exposed to the vacuum of space were sealed with a magnetic field that looked like a giant glowing blue bandage on the hull. Not a full minute after Drex read the last report Ensign Lowell came over the admiral's holoscreen.

"Admiral, the remains of the Eighth Fleet have arrived in system and are forming up with us," Lowell said.

"Thank you, Ensign."

"Yes, Sir," Lowell's hologram saluted.

"Prepare the ship to jump on my command. The Eighth Fleet arrived, and we're all leaving this system together. But we can't stay here any longer. It won't be long until Coalition fleets come to finish us off," Admiral Drex ordered.

The admiral heard Lowell passing orders on to the navigation officer and the ship began to hum as its hyper-drive came online.

Drex knew that the Republic's very survival depended on his ship making it through the day. Not only was the *Kentucky* the last loyal Republic carrier in the galaxy, but it was acting as a mobile base of operations for the Repub-lican government in exile. The fact that the chancellor had made it off New Terra was proof Jeru existed, as far as Drex was concerned. To him, it was a miracle.

It had been drilled into his head since he was a child that the survival of humanity and the survival of the Republic were one and the same. Drex had never once questioned that philosophy, only breathed it. Only embodied it.

The *Kentucky*, carrying *Space Force One* and the *Banshee's Lament*, and the remains of the Eighth Fleet jumped out of the Thurian system together. As far as Admiral Drex was concerned he hoped to never see the system again.

They travelled a short distance through hyperspace, a simple twenty hour journey, to a system within the same sector. The trip had been one of planning and anticipation, rather than rejoicing. Still, whether he admitted it openly or not, Drex was happy to have Admiral Yonk and the Eighth. Had Yonk joined the Coalition he would have proven a formidable foe. As it was, with a battleship and several support ships, the *Kentucky* was in a much better situation tactically.

The plan didn't set too well with Drex. The *Kentucky* needed a lot of repairs. No critical systems were damaged in the blast, but the hull was shattered. The hole in it would take several days to fix, even if there were a shipyard remaining in a loyal system that would be able to service her.

The agenda of the chancellor didn't have any care for what the *Kentucky* did or did not need to function. His plan to strike a blow at the Vargon themselves was bold, Drex gave Krell that much credit. But it was foolish. When Drex put all considerations on the table it seemed like a waste of resources. And resources were one area where they couldn't afford to be wasteful. There was little chance that any weapon they would be able to procure could make a dent against one of the Vargon star-eaters. A vessel the size of a star system, billions of kilometers in length, would not be easy to destroy. A thousand anti-matter warheads would likely do nothing but put a few scratches on one. The thought made a shiver run up Drex's spine.

Admiral Drex watched out the viewport from his quarters as Captain Miller departed in the *Banshee's Lament*, followed closely by Shadow Squadron. He had little hope that the mantids would have anything of real use. But the news that the people of Mantalar were not extinct brought the admiral no small amount of joy. He was emboldened by their survival. He prayed to Jeru that the Vargon defector had something they could use as well.

Things could go very badly. Just as Slaath had, Drex knew he could lose everyone. The mission might just demand such sacrifice of those under his command. He had to fight to get his thoughts to focus on his own task at hand. To forge an alliance with the Drakon Confederation's remaining loyalists. Between the loyalists and the Eighth Fleet the Republic and the Confederation might be able to stand a chance against the Coalition.

But it all came down to Commander Slaath. He'd lost too many already. The entire crew of the *Infernal*, his first officer, the shuttle, and the marines. The only surviving drak on the ship other than Slaath himself was Major Bast. And the Major was still recovering from surgery. Nanobots rebuilt several wounded organs and blood vessels. It was touch and go for many hours, but the Major showed great resilience and pulled through. Drex was reluctant to visit the Commander at the Major's bedside, but didn't see much other choice. The chancellor wanted the alliance forged and he wanted it done yesterday.

Slaath still didn't know who to trust. Intel from the OCR or STARCOM meant little to him, and as such he didn't fully believe the Coalition was behind the destruction of the *Infernal* and not the Confederation. Slaath seemed stuck, some kind of glitch going off in his head that kept him from seeing straight, and kept him from processing the gravity of the situation. Drex was not used to dealing with someone suffering from a mental breakdown. Space Force personnel were treated with a variety of drugs and various types of psychological conditioning, all but ensuring that post traumatic stress had no effect on them. Drex had to keep reminding himself that the Commander did not enjoy the luxury of treatment for his mental health.

Part of him wanted to shove the old lizard out the airlock and be done with it. Slaath had become more of a pain than he was worth. But that part of himself made Drex sick. He often wondered what centuries of military life had done to him. The admiral figured that if he spaced the drak commander then he'd never be able to live with himself. But he had a feeling gnawing at the back of his stomach; one that told him Slaath would bring ruin upon them. Whether the old lizard intended it or not, his mental state was likely to cause any number of reactions from the Confederation leadership. And one wrong move could mean disaster for everyone. For the entire galaxy.

As Drex rubbed his chin he realized that he'd made his mind up. The attempt to forge an alliance with the draks would only suffer if Slaath were part of the talks. The only choice other than actually killing the commander was to have him arrested and thrown into the brig. The thought was weighing heavily on the admiral's mind. Perhaps the best thing to do would be to kill the commander after all. The humane thing would certainly be to put him in the brig, but circumstances were beyond unusual.

Drex was not used to being hung up by command decisions. And not wanting to show weakness in front of his crew, nor in front of the chancellor, he decided to consult with the only man who would understand where he was coming from. Fritz Yonk. Drex and Yonk held the same rank, and had been in the same class at the academy...what seemed like so long ago, on New Terra. Yonk was the only peer that Drex actually had among the survivors.

Ensign Lowell piloted a ship to ship light shuttle usually used for cargo. But the only cargo on board was Admiral Drex. They landed in the cargo hangar of the *Vindicator* and found Admiral Yonk waiting alone on the deck when the shuttle doors opened.

"Good to see you, Vallon," Admiral Yonk greeted his old friend. "Welcome to the *Vindicator*. She's seen better days, but this ol' girl is the finest battleship I've ever seen."

"Good to see you too, Fritz. I have a pressing concern, one that I really don't have anyone else to turn to for advice on," Drex said as he gripped his old friend's hand and pulled him close for a hug.

"Shall we take this to my quarters?" Yonk asked.

"No, I'm afraid this will be a very quick visit. The chancellor expects me to be making a holocall to the Confederation within the hour," Drex said, then sighed deeply. He dismissed Ensign Lowell back to the shuttle before continuing. "The drak commander. Slaath."

"What about him, Admiral?"

"He's lost his damn mind. He was crazy when he

came aboard, and I'd heard for years that he has more than a few screws lose. But the chancellor expects me to use this drak to back me up when calling the Confederation. In my gut I know it's the wrong move," Drex sighed. "But Krell thinks that he, myself, and Slaath can work together to get the Confederation on board. Slaath is like a bull burr-deer in rutting season in a room full of mirrors. He doesn't know up from down, and is likely to cause more harm than good."

"Did you come here to ask me if you should space him?" Yonk just came out and asked. He was very direct like that. In a way that even Drex was not.

"Yes."

"And you are having a moral dilemma because of your complicated past with him?"

"Something like that. And he initiated contact with us. He was the first one to see this all coming, and the first one to try and do something about it," Drex said, hesitant to just accept what his instincts already knew.

"The galaxy is all that is at stake," Yonk laughed. "Space him."

"I..."

"You have to, Vallon. It's the only move. And now that you've told me..."

"Yeah, I know, Fritz. I know. I'll take care of it right away," Admiral Drex said as he turned his back and headed back up his shuttle's boarding ramp. He turned and saluted Yonk before embarking. "Good to see you, Fritz. Glad you made it out of that mess in the Gylian system."

Yonk returned salute and said, "glad to see you too,

Vallon. But hey, you know what this means? Krell gets to make one of us Fleet Admiral."

"Or is it that he *has* to make one of us?"

"I already put in my two cents. I told Krell that you are the man for the job. The finest officer in the whole da…."

"I don't want it. I hope he picks you, old friend."

"And I thought we were getting along so well," Yonk fell into a deep laughter. A moment later Drex followed.

"Hey, Lowell," Drex yelled into his shuttle in a mocking tone. "You want to be Fleet Admiral?"

Both admirals nearly fell down they were laughing so hard. Drex entered the shuttle full of cantankerous mirth, but with a much heavier heart than he wished to have. Killing Slaath wouldn't be easy, not on Drex's soul. But after talking to Yonk he had to admit to himself it wasn't just the right move, it was the only move.

24

The *Banshee's Lament* and Shadow Squadron emerged from hyperspace in the Devorian system. The moon of Devora IV where the Vargon defector was in hiding came into view immediately. The largest moon of a gas giant, it was one and a half times the mass of New Terra. Scanners showed it to be a high gravity world with breathable atmosphere, though no life forms showed to be present.

Miller watched from the canopy of the *Lament*, taking in the view of the surf green planet. It was a beautiful sight to behold. Miller had seen thousands of planets in recent memory, and none were so lovely to look upon. Part of her just wanted to land on the surface and walk off into the alien sunset, never to return. One day. One day she would get the chance to settle down and relax. To live a life of peace and luxury. That is what she kept telling herself.

"I wonder why nobody lives on this rock," Shakedown

said to the squadron. "It's a veritable paradise. Surely the system's on Republic star charts."

"Yeah, about all that...we aren't in Republic space anymore. We're deep into the DMZ. If this part of the galaxy was ever charted, nobody's been here at least since the end of the Great War," Krynn answered.

"I want three birds in the air at all times, watching our backs down there," Miller began issuing orders. "The rest of you Spartans stand watch. If there is anyone on this rock who might be offended by our visit then I want them to see our mechs. They should act as a deterrent."

"Roger that, Captain," Burnout replied.

The *Lament's* scanners didn't show any signs of biological life, but they did show a nuclear power source. There were some very high energy readings coming from deep within a cave, atop a high mountain.

"How are we going to get into the mountain?" Miller asked Krynn.

He searched for a place to land the ship on the mountainside. "Use the neutrino scanner. We should be able to produce a map of the whole place, and assuming it is hollow, or there is a cavern within...well, we should be able to find it. And navigate through it."

Krynn reached past Miller, flipped a switch on the control panel in front of her, and pointed to a screen to her right.

"Oh, I see," Miller replied. "Is there anything this ship can't do, Captain?"

"Not that I've seen yet, and I've seen a lot of..."

Krynn's words were cut off by Burnout's voice breaking over squad comms, "Six bogies have just entered the system. They are in the outer system, but within the Oort cloud. Chances are they know we're here."

"Don't let them draw you away. I have a feeling it's a set-up," Miller said.

"I have a feeling they are miners. That far out in the system, that's the best bet," Shakedown said.

"Good chance of that, Sir," Ensign Ortiz, callsign Pulsar, said. "My parents were miners. They were always out on the fringe of some system, near the Oort cloud."

"Alright, keep an eye on them. If they enter atmosphere, shoot first…shoot to kill," Miller ordered as the *Lament's* landing struts lowered. "We can't take any chances on the Coalition finding us. This may be our one final hope of doing something about…"

And then Miller saw the cave entrance. It was snowing at the high altitude, on the mountainside. She had a hard time seeing it, until the wind took a pause and the snow lightened up. But there it was, not fifty feet from the ship. A massive cave entrance, one large enough to fly several *Banshee's Laments* though. And in the giant portal stood a roughly man-sized being. Something utterly familiar and alien at once. It had two arms, two legs, and a head on its torso. But the head was something like a cross between a fish's and a beetle's in shape. Miller had no doubt that the incredibly strange creature was a robot.

She blinked her eyes, tapped Krynn on the shoulder, and pointed the robot out to him. The weird bot began to wave at them, a greeting Miller assumed. It then beckoned them to join it, motioning for them to exit their ships and follow him into the cave. Krynn simply shrugged, sighed a deep breath, and adjusted his belt.

"XJ-13, you have the ship." Krynn said, putting the bot in charge.

Miller, Krynn, Lemmy, and Kevin departed the ship into the freezing wind that was smashing against the mountainside. While it was only a matter of fifty feet, the walk to the cave entrance was arduous. It seemed to Miller that for every step she took forward, she took two steps back. The enhanced strength her exosuit provided her seemed to make little difference in the high wind. Kevin was having difficulty, leaning in to the gale and pushing his repulsors as hard as they could go.

Krynn, who wasn't a robot and didn't have an armored exosuit, walked directly behind Miller. He let the gale force break around her suit and found some reprieve from its strength in her wake. There was nothing else he could do. Miller's armor told her that Krynn would die within thirty-two minutes in that environment, without an exosuit.

Good thing it only took a few moments to clear the distance to the cave entrance. Lemmy on the other hand had no problems with the wind or cold, tromping along through the blizzard as if it were a gentle breeze.

As soon as they entered the cave's entrance there was no wind, and no cold. It was a pleasant seventy-five degrees. The colossal entry was sealed with a magnetic field that appeared to use the same technology starships used to seal hangar decks and hull breaches from the vacuum of space.

Kevin approached the alien robot first, scanning it with several different conical beams of light of various colors. Miller suspected those were just the ones in the visible spectrum, and that Kevin had probably done a full-spectrum scan across all wavelengths.

The robot did not seem to scan Kevin, or any of them, in return. Nor did it take offense to being scanned itself. It simply waited until Kevin was done, took a deep bow, and in perfect galactic common said, "greetings, Terrans. Welcome to Devora. I have been expecting you."

"Who are you, bot?" Miller asked as Krynn shot her a piercing look. "We didn't come here to parlay with robots. So, if you've been expecting us then you probably know why we are here. So, let's cut to the chase. Were's the Vargon? We need to speak with it, urgently."

"Well, that is a tricky question, now isn't it?" the robot motioned at a series of couches and reclining chairs they had failed to notice. "Make yourselves comfortable. I'd offer you some refreshment, but I don't need refreshment, and therefore have not kept anything on hand. Though I suppose if I had that it would have gone sour by now."

"You sure speak a lot," Miller said, starting to get annoyed.

"Yeah, but it doesn't say much," Krynn chimed in.

The robot gave them a disappointed shake of its head. "What you seek is right before you. You have only to look to find it. Your eyes are open, yet you do not see."

"Not riddles. We don't have frakkin' time for frakkin' riddles," Miller said. Her temper was up and she was getting angrier by the moment.

KV-1N issued a series of beeps and noises. A moment later and Krynn was apologizing profusely.

"Our mistake. I'd very much like to apologize on behalf of myself, my crew, and the Republic," Krynn said as sincerely as he could. He turned to Miller and said, "this bot *is* the Vargon defector, Captain."

"Oh, I see," she replied. Miller hated bots as much as she hated draks. They were argumentative and obstinate at best, and genocidal killers at worst. She'd seen the full gamut. From one side of the galaxy to the other, bots were the most insufferable form of intelligence she'd ever come across. "Well, let's get going then. We can take him with us."

"What were you expecting? Someone a little more...*biological?*" the Vargon asked, though genuine curiosity came through in its voice.

"I thought your race might be fifty-foot squid people. I really didn't know what to expect. But a bot isn't exactly what comes to mind when one thinks of a Kardeshev phase three civilization's citizens," Miller said, brutal with her honesty. "Maybe that is my bias as a *biological* life-form."

"And have you, or anyone of your race, ever encountered a phase three civilization?" the robot asked. "What is, and what you suppose, are often two different things, Captain..."

"Miller. Syn Miller," the captain said as she extended her hand to the robot. To her surprise he took it, and gave her a firm handshake.

"Nice to meet you, Captain Miller. I am...well, your people have never officially met mine. I'm afraid that I do not yet have a name for which to call me," the robot said, an air of sadness in its voice.

"How do you speak our language then?" Krynn asked as he stepped forward and shook hands with the alien bot as well. "Felo Krynn. A pleasure to meet you."

"I have been on this moon for longer than your race has travelled amongst the stars. In that time I monitored the transmissions of many species and got to know many cultures. When first I heard your speech it was seventy-four hundred years ago, by your Terran calendar. A full one-hundred years time after your race first broadcast radio transmissions," the robot explained.

"But we are much farther from Old Terra than one-hundred light years," Miller protested. "That makes no sense."

"Not with your level of technology. No, it would not any sense at all," the robot said as it struck a pose that let everyone know that it had much to say and intended to do so. "You see, the Vargon are masters of space-time manipulating technologies…"

"That's real nice and all, thanks for the history lesson," Krynn cut the Vargon off. "But we have a galaxy to save. Pronto."

"Forgive me. I have been alone on this moon for quite some time. Even one of a race that has no end to its…*lifespan* gets lonely sometimes."

With that they exited the cave and headed back to the ship, bringing the new robot with them. He walked abreast of Miller, helping to shield Krynn from the storm. The storm whose winds seemed to be blowing from every direction at once. Krynn knew that he'd have frostbite in minutes in weather like that, and was thankful that he would be returning to the *Lament* and not crash landed on the world. He'd been in such situations more than once, and survival had never been accomplished prettily, nor easily.

Miller noted that on the short walk from the cave to the ship that the Spartans standing guard over the *Lament* were obscured almost entirely by the driven snow. The winds kept picking it up off the mountainside and whipping it about the peak in a storm that was near total white-out.

When they were safely aboard the ship again Krynn headed straight for the cockpit as Lemmy punched navigation coordinates into the navicomputer. Krynn wanted to jump to hyperspace as soon as they entered orbit. Miller, Kevin, and the Vargon all went to the holochess table in the common area and sat in the chairs around it.

Miller noted how nicely outfitted the ship really was. She'd never really taken the time to notice that it was a veritable luxury ship. *If one is playing a pirate, one had better look as if they had a pirate's tastes*, Miller thought. And most pirates she'd met had one thing in common. They loved luxury. And a holochess table and Verudian carpets screamed luxury. Especially aboard a ship of such small size.

"All right, what can you tell us about the predicament that we face?" Miller asked the robot. "What can you tell us about the Vargon, your agenda, and weaknesses?"

The ship was entering the upper atmosphere and would be rendezvousing with the remaining F-138s of Shadow Squadron in moments. Miller wanted a few questions before they jumped. She was sure that Krynn would come out from the cockpit and take over questioning once they were safely in hyperspace. It was inevitable.

"The predicament you face is one of total annihilation. Total extinction of all life in your galaxy," the robot said dispassionately. "What I can tell you about the Vargon would take millennia just to speak in your language."

"Okay, well…how do we fight them? How do we destroy the star-eating vessel?" she asked, realizing that she really was talking to a bot. No matter how advanced it was, it was still a robot. And talking to robots was Miller's least favorite thing in the galaxy.

"There are many star-eaters, if you are referring to the devices with which stars are taken into our plane. There are millions of them, and in unison they can consume whole galaxies in a matter of months," the robot explained. "I'm afraid that there is no known technology that can destroy them. They are self repairing, self replicating super-structures capable of devouring the very stars themselves. In theory they are not indestructible. However, the destruction of one would require the energy needed to destroy dozens of star systems. The mass of one such super-structure is equivalent to the mass of roughly ten of your New Terran systems."

"The mass of ten systems… And by systems you mean every planet, every asteroid, every comet in them combined…as well as the star?" Miller was shocked that anything contained that much mass, even though she'd seen it with her own eyes. It was like looking at the ocean from the beach. Though it filled her entire view she'd still only seen a tiny fraction of a tiny fraction of the thing.

"I mean every single atom of matter in the system. Down to the particles of dust. Down to the individual atoms of low density hydrogen gas. All of it. The Vargon Empire is all-consuming. All-devouring," the robot said, as sadness crept into its voice again.

Krynn came out of the cockpit. "Glad you got a start on the questioning, Captain," he said to Miller.

"Yes, this robot has been very helpful so far," Miller replied, hoping Krynn wasn't going to say what she knew he was going to say next.

"I know. Me and Lemmy were watching you over the monitors. But there are some things I'd still like to know," Krynn said, gesticulating with his hands. "Like, why did you leave the Vargon? What made you defect?"

"Religious reasons," the bot answered plainly.

"Religious reasons?" Krynn facepalmed. "And I'm supposed to believe that."

"Yes."

"And why should I do that?" Felo Krynn asked, obviously frustrated.

"Because it is the truth Captain Krynn," the robot said. "Now, if you want me to help you I would be glad to do so."

"I want to know about your faith. Indulge me. Give us the quick overview of what the Vargon belief systems are. I've never met a bot that believed in any sort of god before," Krynn said. Miller could tell that he was genuinely curious, though she failed to see how it would help them on a military mission. Matters of faith were something she'd never put any stock in. While many Space Force pilots were followers of Jeru, Miller remained agnostic about religion and didn't care either way; though she did find the sacred texts to be more in line with what she considered mythology than what she considered to be true metaphysical philosophy.

"The Vargon were once a biological race, such as yourselves, though by the time of my birth we had evolved for three-billion years of your time," the robot said as if his mind were in a place long ago and far away. Miller thought of Slaath and wondered if she was seeing her first bot with PTSD. "I was born, in another galaxy, in a universe parallel to this one. When our race faced an extinction crisis as our galaxy was destroyed by a series of supernovae we moved into the space between universes. The shadow between realities the Vargon refer to simply as The Plane."

"Very interesting. But how does religion play into this?" Krynn was getting impatient. "Sorry if I haven't had three-billion years to think about god and/or gods....but we do need to speed this conversation up a bit."

"Forgive my manners," the robot said. "My sense of time, as well as my sense of urgency are vastly different than your own. I would do well to remember that."

"Yes, you would," Miller said, rolling her fingers on the table. "Might as well play a game while we listen to this, Krynn."

"Your'e on, Miller," he said with a toothy smile.

The holochess table lit up at the flick of a switch and the press of a button. Krynn was black and Miller was white. They played in silence while the Vargon spoke.

"We lived on The Plane for aeons. Honing our science to the point where we could break, or make, the laws of physics themselves. We created the star-eaters from the materials we gathered from the two universes. Though the galaxy from which we came was gone, there were still plenty of resources to claim. But it was in this universe that we concentrated our efforts, for it was the richest with resources. And when you looked into the sky with your telescopes and you saw the Bootes Void and all the other great voids throughout the universe…then you saw our work. The emptiness left behind. As our physical forms rotted to nothing over the aeons we honed the ability to transfer our consciousness to fabricated bodies. And then, to power them, to create more of them…our appetite for the energy of suns, and of the materials of entire systems, became insatiable."

"So, how do you power that body then? If you aren't receiving energy from your people's technology any longer," Miller asked, slightly confused.

"To escape my people I transferred my consciousness into this body, as they could not track it. This is an old submersible work-bot from Mantalar. Meant for under-water welding and other deep water projects deemed too dangerous for biologicals. My original robotic form was forty-two feet tall, and was based upon our race's physical form prior to transcendence to artificial bodies."

"What did that look like? I mean, what do the Vargon…or did the Vargon actually look like?" Krynn asked, forgetting entirely about the point of religion.

"We were thirteen to fifteen meters in height by your measurement systems, multihued skin which faded from a grey base to pinks and blues. Most commonly we had orange eyes, though some had blue. Our physical shape resembled an octopus like head with many tentacles atop a vaguely humanoid body. We had two arms that ended in hands similar to your own, but with seven digits and two thumbs...one at the bottom of the hand. We had two other arms which ended in pincher like claws. Ridged, bony spines ran down our backs, and at the tail-bone the spine split into two tails. Each was tipped with a sharp, venomous barb. In your culture we would have been seen as monstrous in appearance."

"Yeah, I think I'm going to have trouble sleeping just knowing what you are inside that bot skin," Miller joked. Krynn laughed.

"And so we found ourselves. Immortal beings who could not truly die. Robots composed of nearly indestructible materials. On the rare occasion when one of us was damaged beyond repair, our consciousness was transferred into another body. Eventually, the Vargon government decided that each and every one of us was to create a hundred copies of ourselves. That our consciousness be put into multiple bodies. And that raised the question..." the robot paused.

"What question?" Miller and Krynn asked in unison.

"If the copies would have souls or not."

"I see. So this is where the religious aspect kicks in," Miller said, smiling. "And you felt they didn't have souls?"

"I knew then as I know now. They have no souls and never will. Thus they cannot truly be alive. By the Vargon definition of life, at least," the robot said, sounding so sad that they expected him to start crying tears.

"And how did that convince you to defect?" Krynn asked, as he put Miller in check with a pawn. "Check."

"I was one of the team of scientists who made the

greatest breakthrough in our race's mighty history of great breakthroughs. We discovered the soul. Even a billion years after the last biologically born Vargon entered existence we searched. And when we found it shockwaves went throughout the Vargon Empire, sparking civil war. Most did not believe they had a soul, and hadn't for longer than they could remember. Others felt vindicated, that their beliefs were validated by science changed the landscape of Vargon society," the robot said, then paused for questions.

"And so why were so many upset to learn they had a soul? Surely it would help your race feel connected to what they once were; to living beings. What was the big deal?" Krynn asked, but Miller saw it right away.

"If we have a soul, then we have an afterlife. Which means there may be consequences for what we do in this life," the robot explained. "And the Vargon had lost touch with what the consequences of their actions were before many of the stars in your galaxy were born. To consume whole systems without a thought to who lived in them… the practice was seen as barbaric by the true believers, as they called themselves. And I was among them.

"The thought of what we'd done to other sentient beings sickened us. To atone for murder was one thing. To atone for genocide another. But we had devoured hundreds of thousands of galaxies. Billions upon billions of stars, and trillions of planets. Our scans told us which ones were inhabited, and which ones weren't. But they all ended up the same in the end. Atomized. Reassembled in rectangular blocks for easy storage. You can't imagine looking at trillions of megatons of carbon blocks, reconstituted from the atoms of living beings across several systems. But I have seen such a sight and been commended by my commanders for creating such product. There is not enough shame, nor enough guilt, in the multiverse for one such as myself. For when I realized that the divine spark inside me was part of a greater whole, and that I'd snuffed out quintillions of such lights for nothing…then I knew true sorrow. True woe. And I led a rebellion that brought the multiverse to all consuming war."

"I take it your cause lost," Miller said as if stating the obvious, rolling her eyes.

"On the contrary. We secured a solid victory and changed Vargon society irrevocably," the robot said.

"So what happened?" Krynn asked.

"We overthrew the old order, but I was too selfless to seize power. I called for democratic elections, a first for our people. And it was our undoing," the robot droned on. "Now, the Vargon are worshippers of death. They utilize technology that lets them not only devour systems, but to harvest the soul-force of all who they destroy. They have become star-vampires in quite a literal sense. They send emissaries among the lesser races before they descend on a galaxy. Emissaries who spread their message of death and rebirth into their collective. I am sure that they have factions in operation in this galaxy already."

"They sure do. Are you telling us that the Coalition, as they call themselves, are part of some galaxy wide sacrificial ritual?" Krynn asked, true consternation in his voice.

"It has been my experience that the leadership of such movements is all that is informed. But this Coalition will be led by those who are hard-line fundamentalist followers of the Vargon," the bot said. "It is, for lack of a better description, a doomsday cult."

"Okay, robot. That will be all for now. We'll get back to this later. I should have had Lemmy jump us out of the system half an hour ago. I really need to get back to the cockpit. Now, is there anything that you want, or anything that I can do for you?" Krynn asked, trying to accommodate their new ally as much as possible.

"Yes, Captain. As a matter of fact there is something which you could easily do for me," the robot said.

"And…what is it?"

"You can kill me."

25

Admiral Drex sat at the table in his cabin half-drunk. He poured himself and Chancellor Krell both another glass of bourbon. One thing that Drex could appreciate about the chancellor was the man's ability to put away spirits. Krell was good and drunk, and Drex was ready to bargain with the man.

"Admiral Yonk thinks I need to space Slaath. He said that it is my duty to do so, and that if I do not then he will come to you with it. He thinks that I have no option other than to kill the drak commander as the old lizard could severely compromise the talks with the Confederation," Drex said, slurring his words slightly. He took a long pull off the bottle, forgetting his glass entirely. "I asked his advice, and that was what he had to say."

"That, Admiral, is not good news," the chancellor said. A series of hiccups interrupted him. "That undermines my plans. Not good. He knows I wanted Slaath at the upcoming talks. And I was about to make him Fleet Admiral."

"That's what he said. That he was going to be Fleet Admiral," Drex said.

"Yeah, well he's got a surprise coming, now doesn't he?" the chancellor laughed. "You know what that means, don't you Vallon?"

"What's that, Jamin?" the admiral played dumb.

"Well you should know," the chancellor broke out into laughter, nearly falling out of his chair as spittle dribbled into his well trimmed beard and tears built in the corners of his eyes. "You're the Fleet Admiral. You're the smart one."

"Thank you, Mr. Chancellor, but I'm afraid I must decline," Drex said, playing humble. "Even if you can't bring yourself to put Yonk in the position, there's got to be a better man for the job than me."

"There is no one else, Vallon. You know that. Like it or not, you are now the only five star officer in the Republic Space Force, Fleet Admiral Drex," the chancellor said.

"Thank you, Sir. I will do my best."

"I need a man to lead us all to hell. By some cruel trick of Jeru, that's you, my friend," the chancellor said, patting Drex on the shoulder as he stumbled up to his feet. "I'm off to sleep this drunk away. When I wake, we will speak with the Confederation. Hopefully by then Krynn will be back. Maybe then we'll have some kind of leverage to pitch them with. If we come to the table with something to offer…"

"Yes, it will make all the difference. I agree," the fleet admiral said.

The chancellor left Drex's cabin and headed down the

corridor to the lift. While there were adequate accommodations on the *Kentucky*, Krell preferred the luxurious comforts of *Space Force One*. Krell couldn't wait to get back to his own space, not after enduring Drex's quarters. The cramped empty room was something that Krell found quite depressing, even as the galaxy crumbled around him.

As he sped down the lift to the hangar where *Space Force One* was docked Jamin Krell's thoughts drifted back to his estate on New Terra. To Monticello. That place named after the artisanal home of a heroic leader from Old Terra, from the dawn of Republican ideals.

Krell chose the name Monticello to remind himself that the legacy of the Republican government began on Old Terra, before the age of exploration. Before humanity had left their home-world to colonize the stars. Monticello, the inside joke that Krell shared with but a handful of beings throughout the galaxy. A few historians of the days before faster than light travel still existed throughout the galaxy, but very few people lived who still knew anything about Old Terra before the first days of the Republic.

The lift stopped, several decks above Krell's destination. The doors opened and Ensign Lowell was standing in the corridor.

"Mr. Chancellor," Lowell said. "I'll take the next lift."

"Oh, no you won't, Ensign. Treat me like anyone else. I'm sure you have somewhere important to be, or something important to do," Krell said, putting in every bit of conscious effort he could not to slur his words.

"Thank you, Sir," Ensign Lowell said as he entered the lift. He went to hit the button for his deck and said, "I see we have the same destination."

"Ensign, do you know about Old Terra? Before the Republic, I mean."

"A little bit, Sir. What in particular?"

"Do you know where the ideals of the Republic come from?" the chancellor seemed deadly serious.

"From before the Great Unification. When humans were divided into many nations. Nations who warred over ideals and resources, constantly," Lowell said.

"Yes. Our ideals are the ideals that survived the Unification. The ideals of the victor. And do you know who that was who seized the reigns of mankind's destiny seventy-five-hundred years ago? The victor, Ensign?" the chancellor asked.

"No, Sir. I'm afraid I do not," the ensign said.

"They were called the Americans. The American ideals of democracy, liberty, and freedom are what the Republic has spread throughout the galaxy," the chancellor said.

The lift was approaching their destination deck. Lowell started to sweat profusely. He rubbed his hands together, a nervous habit.

"Excuse me, Chancellor Krell, but may I ask where you are going with this?"

"Do you know what it was that made the Americans come out on top in the wars for unification? What it was that made them the strongest, the leaders of mankind?" Krell said, darkness in his eyes.

A blade flashed from beneath the sleeve of his exotic overcoat and into his hand. In one fluid motion he raised it and slashed Ensign Lowells throat from ear to ear. As the ensign fell to his knees, clutching his throat in wide eyed surprise and desperately trying to force his life's blood back into his neck, the chancellor continued.

"They did whatever they needed to do to get the job done, Ensign. They seized the initiative, and destroyed their enemies without mercy...offering no quarter," the chancellor said, breaking into a maniacal laughter. "Unlike you Coalition pukes, the Republic actually stands for something, Lowell. Something worth dying for. Something worth killing for."

Ensign Lowell fell onto his side, unable to breath and drowning on his own blood. He tried to reply, to ask for help though he knew none would come. He fumbled with the blaster that he thought he'd concealed so cleverly. And his mind raced, trying to come to terms with what the chancellor had done, and how the man had known, before the lights went out.

"Tell your masters that I'm coming for them, Ensign. I'm sure they'll be able to save you. And when they do, you can tell them how a drunk old man got the drop on you...a Space Force officer...with a knife," Krell kicked Lowell in the gut, causing a gout of blood to spray out of his throat, adding to the pool that covered the lift's floor.

Krell leaned down, found a small rectangular metal box on Lowell's belt and put his fingertip on the button upon its face. He hit the button and stood back. A wormhole tore space-time apart within the lift and sucked Lowell through, who gave a wide eyed and bloody silent scream as he was instantly taken to another place in the galaxy. Where that was, Krell didn't care.

He got out of the lift, turned and looked at the bloody mess on the floor, and said, "God bless America."

26

The jump from the Devorian system to their next destination was quick. According to Krynn's ex-wife, Agent Royce, the mantids and their ship the *Ark* would be in the Cygnaurus system. It was unclear what position the mantids took, but Royce confirmed that they were aware of the situation. Not knowing their position made Miller nervous, but Krynn seemed to take it in stride.

"We knew this was a last ditch effort when we got into this, Miller," he said. "Don't be upset if it doesn't pan out."

Except it was the last chance left to strike back against the Vargon, maybe the only chance they would ever have. Miller took the situation to be much more serious that Krynn did. It shocked her how flippantly he dismissed the destruction of the galaxy.

Lemmy roared in Lyranian, a noise that Krynn obviously understood.

"I see, Lem. This is bad," Krynn said. He turned in

his seat to look at Miller. "Looks like we just jumped into a hot zone. Coalition and loyalist ground forces are slugging it out. Looks like the bugs are down there too."

"Frak! Do we know whose side they're on?" Miller asked. She wanted to ask if they were going to support the loyalist ground forces, but she knew the answer. Their mission was much bigger than simply saving one planet from the Coalition.

Lemmy roared something back over his shoulder. From what Miller could tell, it was several sentences. His lower jaw's tusks glistened in the various blinking and flashing lights of the control panels. Then he chuckled to himself, a thick snorting sound—similar to a horse choking. Miller knew it was bad, but gestured at Krynn demanding a translation.

"He said the bugs are with the Coalition forces, dug in, and making a stand at an overrun Republic FOB. Camp Thunder," Krynn said. "We have direct comm link with the CO of the planetary army, Field Marshall Norga."

"Ok, but why haven't they bombed the site and put the insurrection down?" Miller asked.

"It appears that the chancellor has taken initiative on this one and informed the system governor of the situation. But it is now a stalemate. The Coalition forces are entrenched in a fortified position, and the Republic won't just vaporize them for fear of losing the super-weapon," Krynn said, a candid smile on his face.

"Looks like I'll get to finish what my father started," Miller said.

"And what is that?" Krynn asked, returning to his

instrument panels and piloting the ship into the planet's upper atmosphere.

"Extinction, Captain. I get to finish off the mantids," Miller said, surprised that Krynn didn't immediately pick up on her father's deeds on Manatalar.

"At least this time, the fraks deserve it. Siding with the Coalition…"

"Well it isn't like we offered them citizenship in the Republic. No hive-mind species has ever assimilated…"

"The mantids aren't a hive-mind. They're insectoids, but they are as individual as me or you," Krynn said, a chill running up his spine. It occurred to them both in that moment that Admiral Drex had not known that fact when he ordered the cleansing of Mantalar.

"The first free-thinking insect species we have contact with, and they side with the Coalition. Damn…" Miller said, shaking her head and savoring the irony like a bitter pill.

T he next few minutes were tense, coordinating with ground forces for an assault on Camp Thunder. Neither Miller, nor Krynn liked Marshall Norga. He seemed to think he was running the show, despite Krynn providing an assortment of clearances and executive orders from the OCR. Norga was the kind of man who liked being a big fish in a small pond. And the arrival of Shadow Squadron reminded him that it really wasn't a pond after all that he lived in, but a cave deep within a coral reef in a vast ocean. And the real big fish had come looking for something. Miller was used to dealing with his type. She just hoped that he wasn't some Space Force washout with a chip on his shoulder who'd ended up in charge of a planetary army.

Miller had planed on coordinating a bombing run from the F-138's, piloted by AI, with a full frontal assault led by herself and the other power armored Shadow Squadron pilots. Krynn and the *Lament* would be on standby for extraction, as well as providing air support to the Spartans. But Norga wasn't seeing things that way. He didn't want to commit any of his men to the fighting. Krynn had something to say about that, and was en route to the command outpost where Norga was stationed.

The planet was covered in giant plumes of smoke, black ash filled the sky. The trip from the upper atmosphere to the planet's surface looked like a journey through hell. The *Lament* put down on a field of scorched soil that looked as if it would never harbor life again. There were several fighting vehicles going to and fro, men marching in formation, and sorties of drones launching. There were comm dishes spinning, relay stations buzzing away, and lots of other commotion. But Miller immediately noticed that nothing was actually happening. Everyone looked as if they were working, and working hard at that, but nothing was actually getting done. She'd seen hundreds of such worlds. Run on incompetence, run by incompetents. From one side of the galaxy to the other, fools will be fools.

Miller and Krynn walked to the small plasteel bunker serving as Norga's command post. It made Miller want to puke to see the five-star flag of a Republic Field Marshall flying with the Republic flag and to know that it represented Norga. The man Miller had already judged as incompetent and narcissistic.

Two soldiers approached them, stopped a few feet from them, and saluted.

"Colonel Green, Major Briggs, Cygnaurus Planetary Guard," the older, stockier one of them said as he pointed a thumb at his chest, then at his friend. "Field Marshall Norga already gave you your orders. He won't be receiving you."

"Chancellor Krell doesn't see it that way, Colonel. So, if you would kindly show us to that building right over there..." Krynn pointed at the bunker. "The one with the Marshall's flag."

"Sir, if you don't turn around and get in your ship..." the Colonel was poking Krynn in the chest when Miller's blaster pistol flashed.

In one fluid motion she drew her blaster pistol and shot the colonel right between the eyes. She stood before the Major, the barrel of her J-76 smoking. The T-shaped visor of her power armor's helmet the last thing the colonel saw before he hit the ground. Immediately the Major's demeanor changed.

"Right this way, Captain," he said, barely managing. He was noticeably shaken. Miller and Krynn could both see right away that the man had never seen anyone killed before.

The Major walked into the bunker after the retinal display approved his clearance. Miller followed close behind, her blaster at the base of Briggs's skull. Krynn strutted in behind her, a smirk on his face.

"Stand down!" Major Briggs yelled, as dozens of

weapons were drawn. Every man in the bunker, which was one room, stood from their workstation and pointed their blasters at Miller and Krynn. "This is Captain Miller, of Republic Space Force. There's been some sort of misunderstanding."

The last man to stand was a grey haired, hardened old man with thick, leathery skin. He wore five stars on his collar and epaulets on his shoulders, and smoked a thick stogy. He ashed it, and said, "Welcome to Cygnaurus, Captain. Please forgive Major Briggs. He lacks manners. Something all too common with the locals of this world. Please, have a seat."

Field Marshall Norga motioned to an empty chair, and simultaneously his entire bunker holstered their weapons and went back to their tasks at hand. To Miller it all looked like a bunch of ineffectual calls and paper shuffling, but she sat nonetheless.

She took her weapon off Briggs, who walked out of the bunker shaking and sweating. He'd gone pale, and Krynn laughed at the man on his way out as he walked over to Miller and Norga.

"Look, I know you think you know what is going on here, and you have orders from the chancellor, but the truth is that we will have to live here after. We will have to live here, and deal with the consequences of the day," Norga said.

"Look, chief…" Krynn said, cockiness oozing from him like sleaze from a Valezian pimp. "I know you think your little system is very important…and I'm sure to you that it is. But our concerns…yeah…that's what's really important. There's over a trillion planets in this galaxy, and they may all be gone…and real soon, if we don't succeed in our mission. Now, you can assist us, or you can be declared enemies of the state, and all end up like Colonel —what's his name? The one lying face down on this fried rock you call a planet."

The Field Marshall started to break into a slow laugh, but it was stymied as it started when Krynn's LN-93 found its way right under his chin. A nervous look flashed in his eyes.

Miller stood up, using the megaphone function on her helmet. "Field Marshall Norga is, as of now, relieved of command. Space Force is in command of all operations on this planet, effective immediately."

Krynn marched Field Marshall Norga to the brig. When he returned he found Miller coordinating the coming attack with Norga's command staff. She was relaxed enough to remover her helmet, and seemed to have the respect of the men she was leading. *Good*, Krynn thought.

"Captain Miller, may I have a word with you?" Krynn asked when they seemed to have the plan honed to a science.

"We are ready to execute. We move out in twenty," Miller said, ignoring Krynn.

A few moments later and she walked over to him as the command staff left to prepare their troops.

"Sorry, Krynn. It's been hard to get everyone on the same page. I'm not used to leading such thick headed individuals," she said, shaking her head in disgust. "I have every confidence that we'll succeed though."

"Yeah, I wanted to talk to you about Norga," Krynn

said. "His men seem *very* loyal to him…and that's putting it mildly. I wouldn't be surprised if they pull some serious shit over him. We can't afford to have a coup, not now when…and I'm sure that's how they see it from their side. A coup."

"Well yes, we did just walk in here and start running things. I understand how they see it, and yes, they are resentful. But I impressed upon the leadership that this mission is much, much bigger than they can imagine," Miller said.

"And you trust them?" Krynn asked, half rhetorically.

"No. I don't," Miller replied. A sly smile played across her face for a moment. "That's why I told them that if there's any shenanigans the *Kentucky* and the *Vindicator* will return and vaporize everyone on this rock with positron torpedoes."

"Okay then. Good to see how natural inspiring morale is for you, Captain," Krynn said, trying to play it straight but failing. He laughed so hard that he nearly burst into tears. A few moments later and he was his usual sober, cocky self again. "And should I tie up the loose end then…or not?"

"We can't afford to take any chances at all, Krynn. You know that. Just be discrete," Miller said.

She was hesitant, but knew it was the right move. Norga was just another obstacle in the way. When the galaxy was safe and the Coalition destroyed, then she would feel guilty over such things as the obstacles she'd have to overcome on the way. On that day she would remember the faces of the *obstacles*, but until then she had to bury that. She had to do what needed to be done to assure mission success.

Her power armor sensed that she was feeling anxiety and pumped her full of a cocktail of substances to bring her emotional responses to reasonable levels. She got a signal over squad comms from Krynn. Just a quick three-digit code that let her know that he'd executed Field Marshall Norga.

What a waste, Miller thought. She'd seen a lot of worlds, and known a lot of poor leaders, and Norga was just like all of them. Unable to see past the tip of his own nose, and so used to being in charge that he'd forgotten how to take orders. Ever since the Great War planetary governors encouraged their military leaders to be as independent as possible. The only real result of those policies, five-hundred years later, was a deterioration of the chain of command between planetary and galactic bodies of government. Some planets cared more about planet's rights than they did their status as Republican worlds, and Cygnaurus was one of them.

Miller walked back to the ship as Shakedown landed his bird next to the *Lament*. She loaded up into the fighter-mech, and strapped in to the cargo area. She saw Krynn and gave him a thumbs up. He saluted her, then the cargo door slammed shut and the hull became seamless again. The forward swept wings of the F-138 caught a tiny sliver of sunlight peaking through the scorched sky as it lifted off, making them glisten red. Krynn was reminded of the bloody scythe insignia of Reaper Squadron and a lump caught in his throat.

"All gone. Every frakkin' one of 'em," he said to

himself as he boarded the *Lament*. "And for what? You better make it back, Miller."

Lemmy growled in Lyran, and Krynn just hung his head.

"Yeah, maybe so. And after Royce…I wasn't ready for that. But yeah, Lem. Maybe so," Krynn said, coming to terms with how he felt about Miller for the first time.

27

Camp Thunder was a forward operating base in the wasteland that the local army called *The Scorch*. It was a central tower structure, with a domed top. Fortified positions atop every strategically valuable location along every access road made things more difficult for the ground forces, but that is exactly what Miller and Krynn had planned on. She intended to send them into the meat grinder, to buy her time. Even if they got chewed up.

Miller's plan hinged on the Cygnauran Army tying the enemy up for as long as possible, while Shadow Squadron went in and secured the package. The gut feeling that both Miller and Krynn shared was that it was a trap. That the entire thing was a set-up. Miller reasoned that the bugs' weapon could be moved by the Coalition very easily via their wormhole technology. Krynn had reasoned that it was a trap simply because, "of course it's a damn trap!"

On Miller's mark the operation started. The army fired tons of chaff into the area. Billions of pieces of reflective metals that scramble tracking devices and scanners. Then the Spartans flew in and deployed from their ships just over a small ridge from the FOB. When the troops were disembarked the F-138's commenced an attack run on the enemy positions closest to the tower. Miller needed it to look like she was offering support to the army while leaving the tower and dome intact. She knew the weapon was possibly in there and that any attempt to destroy the building could destroy it.

Three infantry platoons accompanied them on the mission, spread across six armored carriers. A hover tank provided fire support. An artillery battery also provided support from several miles back. If things went south, Miller had them on standby to shell the place with their quad eighty-eights.

Initial scans showed the mantid ship, the *Ark*, was docked outside the tower. Miller had a gut feeling that the weapon was aboard it, but Krynn argued that it was most likely in the tower. Because of this Miller ordered her strike force to forego destroying the mantid ship. She wanted to get close and disable the engines, to make sure that it was unable to jump.

T he first two armored hovercarriers headed west on the main road to the tower, cresting a tall hill just in time to see the Spartans open up on the tower's defense systems. Anti-air batteries exploded in colorful displays as the autonomous craft banked and rolled to avoid incoming fire. The sky erupted around the ships as black clouds of flak blotted out what little sunlight made it to the planet's surface. One of the Coalition cannons got lucky, striking a Spartan directly. Most of the body of the craft disintegrated instantly. The wings and what remained of the fuselage crashed into the tower's dome in a massive explosion, cracking it open like an egg.

Loud cheers went up from the carriers as they watched the Spartans wreck havoc on the traitors. A moment later an auto turret on the adjacent ridge opened up on them. Plasma cannons sent balls of white-hot death through the hull of the first APC, flipping it end over end as it exploded. The smoking wreck gave the men in the second hovercarrier cover as they scurried out of their own lumbering deathtrap before they met the same fate.

The autoturret opened up on them again, and Miller heard the screams of dying men over the Republic channel. "Major, I need a sitrep," Miller ordered over the Republic channel.

"The major's gone, Captain. This is Lieutenant Brak" a young man's voice crackled over the staticky channel. He sounded truly afraid. "We're pinned down by auto-cannons."

"Roger that, Lieutenant. Hang tight. Light up the cannons with a spotting laser if you can. Airstrike is inbound," Miller said. *Good, their buying us time*, she thought.

Miller watched the battle unfold over her HUD as the Spartans lit up the ridge, then rocketed off to make another pass of the battlefield, and the soldiers got under way again. The five remaining troop transports continued from the north, east, and south. Coalition artillery rained hell down around the hovercarriers, but they pressed on with determination.

The repulsor tank stayed positioned on the ridge, next

to the wrecked APC. As the soldiers advanced it fired upon the the tower's autodefenses. Miller wanted to create the illusion that they were trying to drive the enemy from their position with overwhelming force, and ordered a direct frontal assault on the tower. Shadow Squadron crouched in a ravine full of boulders and jagged rocks, south-southwest of the tower. The chaff and flak rendered the enemy scanners inert long enough for them to get into position to assault the *Ark*.

Krynn's voice came over the squad channel. "Miller, I have confirmed that the mantids are holding the weapon aboard the *Ark*. The tower is not the target."

"Roger that, Krynn. And do we know why they haven't just jumped the weapon out of system via worm-hole?" she asked as she checked the charge on her blaster.

"Yes. The weapon itself *is* a worm-hole generator. To send it through a worm-hole could possibly destroy the universe," Krynn said. She could tell he wasn't exaggerating.

"Did you get this from the Vargon?" Miller asked as she noticed a wave of Coalition footsloggers pouring out of the tower.

"Yeah, he figured it out. Along with Kevin. Its like those bots were made to work together," Krynn said, as the *Banshee's Lament* strafed the tower dome with its mini-guns on a flyby. The structure was ready to collapse in on itself, the roof spider-webbed to the point of no return.

Miller gave a signal and Shadow Squadron used the jump jets in their power armor to ascend the ravine. They hit the ground running. Three units of three. Valkyrie, Shakedown, and Burnout each leading.

Miller found herself with a clear line of sight to the first wave of enemy troops. They were moving forward to engage the army and were ignoring her troops completely. *Good*, she thought. *They haven't gotten their scanners back online.* It wouldn't have mattered much if they had. The power armored exosuit had many stealth capabilities built into its passive systems. Miller and her Spartans were undetectable by infrared and microwave scans.

She raised her blaster and unloaded her charge pack, her armor's AI choosing targets for her as fast as she could fire. Ten Coalition fighters dropped dead, the rest still unaware of her position. It would make the enemy upset enough to do something stupid, and stupid was what she needed in that moment. If she could keep the Coalition and the Cygnauran Army reacting to one another's mistakes then she might be able to pull off her mission during the confusion.

"Move!" she ordered her squad, Burnout and Shakedown taking their own routes to the ship.

They ran across what was essentially open ground, using the sparse boulders for cover when they could. Miller halted and went down on one knee, and popped open the holoscreen on her forearm. A moment later and she was on the move again, confident that there were no mines or traps along the way. It made her uncomfortable that the *Ark* was virtually undefended.

A loud *crack!* shattered the sky, and Miller knew that without her helmet's audio filters that she'd be deaf. Even with her helmet on it was nearly enough to make her jump in her skin, its audio buffers stressed to their limits. Another of the AI controlled Spartans was hit by anti-aircraft fire, and hit the ground in a spectacular fireball. It felt like an earthquake, and even with her armor's gyroscopic stabilizers she was a bit disoriented.

Miller was shocked that two birds had already fallen. She wasn't used to being so long outside of the cockpit of her Spartan. She had to fight to push the thought of Lionel out of her head and focus on the task at hand.

"Damnit, that's my second one this year…" Burnout said. "Looks like I'm a footslogger now, like you, Miller!" He laughed as they sprinted toward the *Ark* at superhuman speeds.

Though they dare not use jump-jets they were able to close the distance with ease. Miller felt it best to maintain as low a profile as possible. The shipyard was sparsely populated with single-man surface skimmers and in-atmosphere aircraft. There was one frigate, from the First Fleet, that Miller did not immediately recognize. Her HUD couldn't tell her what ship it was as the Coalition had made many adjustments to the vessel, as well as changing all identifying markers to a mixed Terran-Drako hybrid system which Miller had never seen.

Her scanners showed no signs of life aboard any of the ships in the shipyard, except for the *Ark*. The battle around the tower grew more intense as the Spartans waged war on the ground in mech-mode, and lead the army past the inner perimeter defenses.

"Captain Miller, we are pushing 'em back. We'll be breaching the tower in no time, Sir," Lieutenant Brak's voice came over the Republic channel.

"Good work, Lieutenant. Hoorah!" she shouted, using the local army's battlecry.

"Hoorah, Sir!"

A moment later and the green dot on Miller's HUD that represented Brak disappeared, replaced by a red unmoving X. From the looks of it, he took a direct hit from a mortar round. The kill zone centered on Brak, but Miller saw eight green dots turn to five red, and three yellow X's.

"Jeru, forgive me," she absentmindedly said aloud into the squad comms. "They're getting chewed up."

Another Spartan fighter-mech fell to combined, focussed fire from shoulder mounted grenade launchers. The cyclopean robot crashed to the ground, and kicked up a cloud of dust and ash. Miller watched on the HUD as enemy forces swarmed over the bot to assault the loyalist soldiers, some taking up firing positions behind the wreck.

Miller and her teams were within a dozen meters of the *Ark*, converging on it from three sides. She noticed an anomaly on the scanner, it fuzzed out and gave no reading. When it came back online there were no lifeforms showing on the ship except one. A few hundred mantids were gone. They didn't show up in the melee or in the tower, and Miller assumed that they left via wormhole.

She turned to wave her squad onto the loading ramp of the Ark, which was down and unguarded. Even if it weren't a time of war any ship its size would have personnel guarding the vessel. It was quite unusual that there was no one.

"We're going in," she said to the other Shadow Squadron members. "But I've got a bad feeling about this. Stay sharp."

She took a step onto the ramp and heard the squad's

reaction as Pulsar's head exploded, hit by a hypervelocity rail-gun shell. Chunks of skull and helmet sprayed over Miller.

"Sniper! Move!" she screamed. "Ortiz is KIA."

The squad hustled up the ramp, but Burnout took a slug in the hip. A lucky shot, or a good sniper, hit him between the armored plates of his suit. Lieutenant Jaxon, callsign Raygun, grabbed his wrist and pulled him up the ramp. Another round glanced off Burnout's boot before he was safely aboard the *Ark*.

"He's bleeding bad, Sir," Raygun said.

But Miller already knew how bad it was. Burnout wouldn't be able to walk, or so her HUD said. But he wasn't in danger of dying. The nanobots in his suit were already repairing the wound. Miller was glad it was a slug that hit him, and not another rail-gun shell, but her HUD told her that he would need a new hip if he ever wanted to walk without a limp.

Raygun propped Burnout up into a sitting position and helped him get his rifle situated. Miller stepped over and said, "Burnout, anybody comes up that ramp that you don't recognize...you dust 'em."

"Yes, Sir!" Burnout said. Miller could tell by the sound of his voice that the suit had already pumped him full of general pain medication.

Captain Miller turned and examined the interior of the alien ship. Many of the surfaces were composed of the strange green crystal that Admiral Drex kept in his quarters. Occasionally a pulse ran through the ship and the crystals rippled with various colors. There was a corridor before them, with many others branching off to the sides.

But at the end of the main corridor was a door. Captain Miller motioned her squad forward and the door opened. It appeared to be a lift.

They walked to the lift door, which seemed to be much farther away than the ship was long. Two of the power armored Republicans, Raygun and Rattlehead, took up positions on either side of the door. The rest entered the lift. There appeared to be no control panel, but the door shut behind them and they rocketed to the upper decks in a flash. Miller was impressed by their technology. The lift moved so fast that they would have normally been smashed if they were not in power armor. But her systems showed no signs of increased G-forces. *They are easily able to harness high levels of energy and manipulate them as they see fit. Even their lifts have inertial dampeners*, Miller thought.

The lift doors opened into what appeared to be a throne room of some sort. It was extremely alien, though opulence emanated from every surface. The floor was covered in an exotic carpet of strange design and unknown material. There was only a walkway to the seat and room to stand on either side of the aisle.

The throne itself was one solid aquamarine beryl, and Miller's HUD told her that it originated on Old Terra. Upon the seat sat a mantid in a red silk robe. It appeared somewhat larger than others of its species, and much older than Miller imagined they could live to be. It was albino, and its skin was cracked and dull all over. Captain Miller did not know the mantid race well, but she knew that the being she was looking at was dying. The hunched over old bug beckoned them forward with a single finger-like appendage on the tip of its right arm. Miller wondered if she was looking at a mantid queen.

A bot emerged from behind the throne, the same make as the Vargon defector used, and projected a hologram from its eyes into the air between the squad and the mantid. It played a short clip illustrating what the super-weapon was and how it worked.

Miller watched to see a small mantid frigate jump through hyperspace, and come out inside the heart of a star. The ship withstood the tremendous pressure for a few moments, pushing its shields to their limits. Then the view shifted to within the ship, where a bot pressed a button on a device which looked similar to the Coalition's wormhole generators. Space-time was torn apart inside the ship as a wormhole opened. A wormhole which led to another star. The ship was crushed as the second star entered, consuming the hydrogen that fueled the first star in an instant, and blowing the system apart in a supernova.

The hologram ended, and the old bug motioned Miller to come forward. She took the first step, and the second, but by the third she was already asking questions.

"So, you can pull a nova into another star…and cause a supernova explosion?" Miller wondered, more to herself than the mantid.

It nodded at her in the affirmative. The bot's vocal speakers crackled as they came online. It had not used them in a long while.

"Yes, Captain. And we leave this power with you, though it is against our better judgement," the bot said on behalf of the mantid. "We have foreseen the future,

Captain Miller. It is you who will save our galaxy from the clutches of oblivion. And you will need this."

"Then why did you side with the coalition?" Miller asked, perplexed. Her HUD showed her that the battle outside was not going well for the local army. They were in full retreat, and the four F-138 Spartans that remained left the battlefield, waiting with Krynn to extract Miller and her team. The tank, which had shelled the tower to ruin, covered the army as it fell back.

The bot played another hologram. It showed the mantid queen in the very room they stood in. The whole of her people, had voted against her, siding with the coalition. Instead of trusting their queen's prescient visions, as they had for millennia, the last survivors of Mantalar's great race chose to disregard tradition. They chose hubris. They chose to treat the ways of their people as based in nothing but myth and legend.

And she chose to vaporize them all, at once, ending the entirety of her people. It had all happened moments before Shadow Squadron boarded the *Ark*.

"The galaxy is more important than any one race, Captain. Certainly the human, drak, grund, or even mantid races. You would have never gotten the device, Captain, had Queen Zorra not destroyed her people. And then all races would be gone. Erased from existence," the bot said.

The sound of blaster fire came over the squad channel. Burnout screamed in pain, the shockwaves of an explosion rippled throughout the ship. Seconds later and he was just another red X on her HUD. The two troopers at the bottom of the lift opened fire on a mob of human and drak soldiers who were coming up the ramp.

"We've got company, Captain," Rattlehead shouted.

Miller turned to the robot. "Can you fly this bird out of the hot zone, bot?"

"Yes, Captain Miller," the robot said. "I can pilot it remotely, as my AI is shared between this body and the shi…"

"That's nice, bot! Just get us out of here!" Miller screamed, taking all the frustration she'd ever felt toward bots out on it.

"Closing loading ramp doors. Initiating take-off. What is our destination, Captain?" the bot asked.

Miller gave him the longitude and latitude of the rendezvous point. She then switched to the Republic channel to issue orders to the Cygnauran Army, and was not surprised to see that they were all dead. Even the tank was a smoking wreck. She switched to the squad channel.

"Krynn. We are inbound, aboard the *Ark*. We have the package," Miller said. "Mission accomplished."

"Roger that, Captain," Krynn replied. "Get here asap. We've got orders to return to the *Kentucky*."

"Confederation didn't want to forge an alliance, did they?" Miller said, laughing a bit to herself. "This might have all been for nothing in the end…"

"Something like that, Captain. Something like that."

"We have a wounded man. He's stable, but he's going to need serious attention. Have XJ-13 on standby," Miller said. "Oh, and one more thing. Do you have any nukes or heavy ordnance aboard the *Lament*?"

"I have a couple of positron torpedoes. Why?" Krynn asked, though he knew the answer.

"We're blowing Camp Thunder from orbit, and I'm going to watch it burn as we leave this frakkin' system," Miller said.

"Roger that, Captain."

Admiral Drex was trembling in his anger, barely able to pour the chancellor a third bourbon. They sat alone in his quarters, trying to drink away their worries and failing miserably. The last desperate attempt at saving the Republic fell on its face. And Drex had no one to blame but himself. Himself and Commander Slaath.

"I told you the old lizard was crazy, but I really had no idea," Drex said, then hiccuped. "Yonk was right. And now I'm eating crow...but you wanted him too, Mr. Chancellor...if I recall."

"This is no time to beat ourselves up about the past, Vallon. Besides, this might all work itself out in the end. I mean, if Miller and Krynn get back with the package... well, we might just see ourselves out of this mess," Krell said. "And then we'll deal with the Confederation...the ungrateful fraks."

"I wouldn't trust us either," Drex said. He took a deep pull off his bourbon, and continued, "and in the name of

Jeru…I had no idea that Slaath had frakked President Cyrex's wife."

"I don't think Slaath did either," the chancellor chided.

A beep came from his wrist and he raised his watch up, a hologram of his android wife Max appeared.

"Darling, agent Royce has just received urgent news from her source within the Coalition. She's still communicating with her source, but says she needs to see you immediately," Max said, trying to sound sexy for Krell even when delivering news.

"I'm drunk, honey. Send her up here when she's done."

"But I was looking forward to seeing you, baby," Max said, pursing her perfect lips at him.

"Then bring Royce up here. Okay?" Krell said, impatiently. "You can see me then, sweetheart."

"Okay, ciao!" she said. The hologram closed.

"You hear that, Drex?" the chancellor asked. "Royce has critical intel about the Vargon. I told you this would all work out."

"You sure are confident, Chancellor."

"You've got to be when you're in my position. There's no other option," the chancellor said. He took a big pull off his bourbon, trying to outdo Drex. "The masses are jackals, Vallon. And they will devour you the moment you show *any* weakness. Don't forget that, my friend."

A hologram appeared over the projector on Drex's table. It was Commander Crom, and he looked disappointed to see the two most powerful figureheads of the Republic-in-exile hammered drunk.

"Admiral Drex, we have received word that the mission was a success. Shadow Squadron is en route home," Crom said.

"Any losses?" Drex asked, casually sloshing his drink around in his glass.

"Yes, Sir. Four KIA. Five F-138's lost," Commander Crom reported without any emotion.

"Who, Commander? Who did we lose?" Drex demanded. He poured himself another glass. "I don't care about the whats…it's the who's that matter."

"Pulsar, Burnout, Rattlehead, and Raygun, Sir," Crom answered.

"That will be all, Commander." Drex closed the hologram.

"Did you know those men well, Admiral?" the chancellor asked.

"I know everyone under my command. And my pilots…personally, Jamin," Drex said as stoically as he could manage. "Burnout was best-man at my son's wedding."

"I'm sorry, Vallon," Krell said, pouring himself another glass. "Really, I am. When it hits close to home…"

"Yeah…I know, Jamin. I know," Drex said. "But there's no time to mourn the dead. Not today. Not while we're at war."

"Then let's put an end to this," Krell said. "Let's end this and rebuild from the ashes, as humanity has always done."

Before Drex could respond the computer alerted them that Max and Agent Royce had arrived, and were waiting outside the door. Drex pressed a button and the door opened, the computer's robotic voice welcomed them in.

"Darling, so good to finally get to see you," Max said, sitting on the arm of Krell's chair and kissing him on top of his head. She smelled his thick black hair and sighed.

"Good to see you too, dear," Krell said, then turned to Royce. "What do you have for me, Agent?"

"The Coalition fleets are gathering, in the Talari system, in thirty-six hours they will declare martial law throughout the galaxy," Royce reported. Drex poured her a drink.

"What about the Vargon?" Drex asked.

"Sir, the Talari system is their next target. The Coalition has been stripping the primary planet's resources for weeks. Valdana wants all Coalition fleets to witness the destruction of the system," she said. Royce then took a sip off her bourbon, savoring the taste on the back of her tongue. "Michter's?"

"I see you know your bourbons," Drex said. "But this is exactly what we needed to know. Where they're going to be, and when they're going to be there."

The chancellor pushed his wife away as she struggled to continue showering him with kisses. "The only problem is that the Coalition will be there, in full force."

"I thought you were mister confidence," Drex said, falling into drunken laughter and nearly out of his chair.

"Confident that we can use the bugs' weapon… possibly put an end to, or slow down the destruction of our galaxy. But that was before I knew Valdana would be there," the chancellor said, agitated. He started to sweat, and the volume of his voice increased. "We're going to hit them another time, *Fleet Admiral*," he said.

"Don't threaten me, Krell," Drex deadpanned. "This isn't the time for it. We might not get 'another time' to hit these frakkin' bastards. I'm willing to sacrifice every ship in this rag-tag fleet to save the Republic…"

"Are you suggesting that I'm soft? *You?*" the chancellor demanded. "A man under *your* command tried to assassinate me in the lift, my friend."

"Boys, please. Don't fight. You are friends," Max said in a voice designed to decrease tension and hostility in human males.

"Agent Royce, thank you for your report. Would you see the First Lady back to *Space Force One?*" he asked, though it wasn't a question.

"Of course, Chancellor," she answered. "Right away."

It was a few minutes after Max and Royce left the room before either man spoke. "We strike while the iron is hot, Jamin. That is my military decision. But you have a point, and I need to hear you out. This is not the kind of decision to be taken lightly," Drex said.

"I concur, Vallon. And I apologize. Now, pour me another glass of that Michter's bourbon," Krell said.

They sat in silence, sipping whisky for some time. Krell finally took a very deep sigh, sounding as melodramatic as his android wife, and stood up. "Look, Drex," he said. "I can see what you're saying. This is the only shot that we know for sure that we will ever get. We *have* to take it. I just wish there was another way."

"But there's not. Often in politics your kind, and I mean no offense, has another way," the admiral said.

"Multiple avenues of approach allow you to overcome the situations you face. But here…now…this is it. We win, or we die. And if we win, we face a galaxy of traitors…"

"Yes, this is also true. Valdana rules the galaxy, with all the might of the fleets behind him. And I…we…well, we've got little of nothing going for us," Krell said.

"Nothing but ideals," Drex reminded him. "Ideals which have withstood the test of time for seventy-five hundred years."

"Funny you say that, Admiral. I gave Ensign Lowell quite the speech about Old Terra, specifically ancient America, as he bled out in the lift."

They both had a good laugh about it, then the computer informed Drex that the *Banshee's Lament* and the remaining Spartans of Shadow Squadron had returned. The two men sobered up a bit by the message, but were too drunk to really take it seriously.

"To Shadow Squadron" the chancellor raised his glass to toast their bravery.

"To the fallen," Drex said, clinking his glass into the chancellor's before pouring half his drink on the floor.

"Drex, we better sober up before we do this," the chancellor said. "There's only thirty-six hours…look, I don't want to be hung over when we do this…"

29

Miller couldn't believe the plan that her father had come up with. It was one thing to face the Coalition fleets, but to face them all at once was suicide. She had advocated for a plan of action which required only one ship to enter the system, and set off the device. It would inevitably be destroyed in the process, but Drex's plan was going to get them *all* killed as far as she was concerned.

"Better we die than we fail," he'd told her. She really couldn't argue with the logic in theory, but in practice it was suicidal. Drex's main concern was that the Coalition see them as making a foolish attempt at a last stand, to distract the real threat. If anything tipped the Vargon off, or the Coalition for that matter, then the enemy would know their intent. The chancellor agreed with Drex. The only way to get the job done was to make it look authentic. They had a very narrow window in which to get the mantid device into the heart of the Talari star.

Miller didn't disagree with the decision militarily, but

she knew it wasn't going to be pretty. If anyone was left standing to remember them perhaps they'd be considered heroes by future generations. It made her sick to her stomach as she prepared to launch from the main deck of the *Kentucky* in the new F-138 Spartan she was issued.

It was a new bird, but Lionel was already installed, and configured to her specs, just as Chief Brudly knew she'd appreciate. The master mechanic was the best at his job, and Miller was always thankful when he was the one servicing her bird.

The Coalition was already in system, but by their formation it was apparent they were there to spectate and did not expect to be assaulted by the remnants of the Republic. Miller knew many of the ships' commanders personally. Many had been her students at the academy.

The launch was smoother than usual, Miller noted as she zipped off the flight deck. She flew off toward the Coalition fleets, who were several light-minutes away, on the opposite side of the system. The Talari star between them. Shadow Squadron formed up on Miller as a swarm of AI piloted drone fighters launched behind them, two hundred in total. The plan was to sow disruption and confusion while the *Vindicator* and its support ships closed with the enemy.

The last part of it all, and the part which Miller disliked the most, was to jump the *Kentucky* into the heart of the star and engage the mantid super-weapon. It was the only ship they had with shields that would last long enough. Any other vessel, even the *Vindicator*, would be smashed immediately. The *Kentucky's* shields would only last moments, but it would be long enough to engage the super-weapon. The timing had to be perfect, but if they could pull it off when the Vargon engaged their star-eater...then they would be eating a supernova explosion. It was the only hope that remained. A desperate, last ditch effort. They were playing for the fate of the galaxy, but the Vargon did not hold all the aces.

Miller wasn't used to Shadow Squadron being so... small. With only herself and four other Spartans she was determined for them all to make it home. And if the *Kentucky* was able to destroy the Talari system's star they would have to jump into hyperspace at a moment's notice.

"One minute to contact, Shadow Squadron," Miller said. "Concentrate fire on the corvettes and frigates. We won't last long against the destroyers or battlecruisers."

"Roger that, Valkyrie," Shakedown replied. "Let's give 'em hell."

"Don't forget, this is a distraction. Make it look good, but you don't need to take any chances. Nobody needs to do anything stupid," Miller replied. "We're all heroes today...all of us. Everyone makes it home!"

But she knew that wasn't true. It would take a minimum of twelve crewmen to jump the *Kentucky* into the heart of the star. Commander Crom and Admiral Drex had argued over who was going to be the one to remain and command the ship, and who would be going to the *Vindicator*.

As much arguing as there was it was nothing compared to the argument over Chancellor Krell remaining to fight alongside the Republic forces from *Space Force One*. It was not outfitted for war, but Krell insisted. Drex and Yonk both agreed that the chancellor should stay out of the system, at the rendezvous point. It nearly took a military coup to convince the obstinate chancellor that his safety was of the utmost importance.

When the day was over, and the battle done, the Republic would need a figurehead...a point to rally around and rebuild. Yonk and Drex both saw Krell as not only the obvious choice, but the only choice. He was proof positive himself that the Republic still lived. Once Drex explained it to him in such terms Krell conceded.

The Coalition fleet was a sight to behold. The First Fleet, the Sixth Fleet, the Ninth Fleet...all in their entirety, alongside just as many drak ships. It was the largest collection of starships Miller had seen since the Great War, and the most she'd ever seen that were part of the same fighting force. The sight was awe inspiring. Captain Miller wished that it was the Republic and Coalition that had come together in peace, rather than extremist splinter factions of both.

The Coalition fleet seemed to pay them no mind. *And why should they*, Miller thought. *They outnumber us a hundred to one.* Shadow Squadron, or what was left of it, pushed their sub-light engines to their limits. They tore across the system, drones in tow, to wreck havoc.

"Watch out for minefields," Miller said. "We don't want to end up like Reaper Squadron."

"Roger that, Valkyrie," Ensign Moth, callsign Warpig said. "Scanners show we are in range of their battleships."

"Confirming incoming rail-gun fire from Coalition battleship. Take evasive action," Captain Miller said. The realization that they'd have to endure another minute of fire from the Coalition fleet before their own weapons were in range made Miller's stomach do a backflip. A moment later the exosuit was pumping an anti-nausea medication into her bloodstream.

Rail-gun rounds were easily avoided at such astronomical distances, and the Coalition fleet was firing simply for good measure, and to make a point. But it wouldn't be long, a matter of seconds before they were in range of the traitor fleet's battle cannons, torpedos, missiles, and quad batteries. The system was about to light up in a multicolored display of fireworks.

And right on queue, as predicted, the ordnance came. Drone fighters swarmed ahead to take the brunt of the attack, their laser weapons rendering as many of the incoming missile's electronic systems obsolete as they could. But still the missiles kept coming. A drone flew ahead of the rest of the strike force, detonated itself and spread a wide field of hot metal across the area. Many of the incoming missiles detonated against the scorching chunks of the shattered ship.

The drones did their best to shield the incoming fire, but Shadow Squadron still had to do plenty of shooting. They made it into weapon's range with only half the drone fighters that had left the *Kentucky*, but lost none of the Spartans.

The hubris of Admiral Valdana was apparent to Miller immediately. He treated their attack with contempt, not even taking it seriously enough to launch fighters. He intended to shoot them all down while his fleet sat back and watched the Vargon eat the system.

Miller knew what ship Valdana would be on. And she knew that the plan of attack they were executing was exactly what he anticipated. So she decided to alter the plan, on the fly.

"Change of plans, Spartans," Miller said. "We're taking down Valdana."

"Roger that, Captain," Lieutenant Gorsch, callsign Shockwave, said.

Miller punched in a few keystrokes on the control panel in front of her and a moment later the remaining fleet of autonomous drones was given a new target. They shot through the traitor fleet, passing every ship by until they arrived at the former flag ship of the Republic Space Force. The supercarrier *Montana*.

By the time the drones made it to the flagship there were only eighty-two of them left. Miller watched over a POV holofeed as they unloaded every missile pod they had, all into a single point on the *Montana's* hull. The bombardment did little to the enormous capital ship, but it crippled her shields. And into the same point the drones smashed themselves. One by one. Each detonating its onboard fusion reactor. Seventy-five drones in total made it to impact, as the entire fleet's guns tried desperately to shoot them down when someone realized the grave mistake they'd made.

"Valdana was always a fool and a narcissist," Miller said as she watched the *Montana* buckle, a two-kilometer wide crater in its hull.

A moment later and the super-carrier tore itself apart. Wrenched in half it smashed into a battleship and a destroyer. Flames several miles long poured from the ship before the airlocks sealed, the crew's oxygen consumed in a flash. Escape pods and shuttles flew from the carcass of the largest ship the Republic had ever built.

Shadow Squadron closed for the kill, taking advantage of the moment of confusion. "Prioritize the shuttles," Miller said. "If Valdana lives he's more likely to be aboard a shuttle than in one of the escape pods."

"Sir, shooting down escape pods and emergency shuttles is considered a war crime under section…" Warpig said, before Miller cut him off.

"This isn't a war, Ensign. These are traitors to the Republic. And what do we do with traitors?"

"We execute them, Sir!" Shakedown chimed in.

The squadron remained at maximum velocity, burning past the smaller ships of the traitor fleet so fast they hardly had to avoid any incoming fire. Before the enemy could respond they were flying beyond one ship and coming to the next one. In seconds the squadron was upon the shattered hulk that had been the *Montana*. Miller knew the psychological effect that such a blow would have had on the enemy, and she intended to utilize their emotional state against them.

"Shock and awe," Miller said. "Now we clean up the rest of this trash."

She locked onto the first shuttle that appeared on her HUD and fired a salvo of positron torpedoes at it. Antimatter rounds were overkill for such a small ship, but she wanted to make a point. You betray the Republic, and you get vaporized. One after the other Shadow Squadron chewed through the pods and shuttles, only a few making it to the safety of other ships. Miller hoped that she'd killed Valdana, but even if she hadn't she'd managed to land a crippling blow to their morale.

"Drak fighters, incoming. Eight o'clock high!" Shockwave said. "They finally want to fight."

"Then we'll give them a fight!" Miller screamed, thirsty for blood.

Before the enemy closed with them the squadron's scanners picked up the Vargon star-eating superstructure emerging from hyperspace. It began to surround the star, and Miller knew the time had come.

The first of the drak fighters came at Warpig, calm and cool. It didn't even fire until it was close enough that the pilots could see one another through their canopies. It rolled away from Warpig's miniguns with ease. And when it was right on top of him it lit him up with the wing-tip mounted rail-guns that gave the drak fighters such a sinister appearance. A hypervelocity depleted uranium shell smashed through Warpig's canopy and exploded through his chest and into the back of his fighter. He was pulped inside his exosuit, never even feeling the pain of being turned to goo. The Spartan erupted into a fireball, and crashed into a chunk of the shattered *Montana*.

"Warpig!" Shakedown screamed as he squeezed the trigger on his stick, firing wide across the front of the drak fighter as it rolled away. Eleven others fell into formation with it.

"Looks like these guys know how to fight," Miller said, completely unfazed by the loss of Warpig. She knew that if she lived through the day that there would be time to mourn, but in the moment, even thinking about it could get her killed.

"Hotshot, Shakedown, break off on three," Miller ordered. "Let's double back and see if we can't get some of them to follow us. Hit 'em with the crossfire."

"If we time it right…just don't blast us, okay?" Shakedown asked. He was not confident in the plan, and it showed.

"Three!" Miller said, cutting right with Shockwave. Hotshot and Shakedown cut left and dove.

The enemy fighters divided into two groups and fell in behind the Spartans, struggling to get a firelock on the Republic fighters as they turned tight and hard, their ion engines still pushed to their limits. The G-forces nearly caused Miller to black out, despite the Lockheed One-G system all Spartans were fitted with. Between the inertial dampeners, and the exosuit, she was supposed to feel nothing. But her eyeballs felt like they were going to turn to jelly. Like everything else in the Republic, it worked better in theory than in practice.

When Miller had nearly completed an entire three-sixty turn she saw Hotshot and Shakedown and fired every rocket she had across their wake. Shockwave fired his rockets along with hers, dozens in total. Each one found the enemy fighters, and all six were wiped out in an instant. Hotshot and Shakedown banked hard to fall in behind the ships pursuing Valkyrie and Shockwave.

Captain Miller had found the perfect moment to fire off her missiles, as had Lieutenant Gorsch, but Hotshot and Shakedown were not able to get into firing position. The maneuver would have been tricky even if they'd practiced it every day for months. Miller didn't like that it was only partially successful, but she knew it was a longshot.

Still, six on four was much better odds than twelve on four.

And then Shockwave's Spartan exploded, hit by a drak plasma cannon. He was gone in a flash as the plasma tore into the Spartan's ion engines. A rapid chain-reaction of explosions consumed the ship, and left behind little of nothing. The drak pilot was lucky with his shot, and it sent Miller into a blind rage.

It was pure luck which kept her from doing something stupid, as Admiral Drex's deep voice boomed over the fleet channel. If she hadn't heard her father issue her orders in that very moment, Miller knew she would have gotten herself, and the remnants of Shadow Squadron, killed.

"Good work, Captain. Initiate phase two," the admiral said.

Miller signaled her squadron to jump back to the fleet, a short in-system hop through hyperspace. She wanted to smash her flight controls in anger knowing that the drak fighters would get away from her, though smiled from ear to ear at the thought of phase two.

Shadow Squadron jumped out in a flash. They engaged their hyperdrives when in close proximity to a drakon destroyer, shredding the starboard hull to pieces. Equipment and personnel were blasted out into space as the ship listed.

The moment that Shadow Squadron formed up with the Republic's patch-work fleet the mantid ship, the *Ark*, jumped into the heart of the Coalition fleet. Drex had watched as the last living mantid, Queen Zorra, perished. He held her hand in her dying moment, promising that her last batch of eggs would be looked after. She told him that she trusted no one else with the future of her species. And the admiral had never been so humbled. Drex didn't have the heart to tell her that he wouldn't be around to see them hatch, to make sure they grew to adulthood.

The mantid bot piloted the ship, in her honor. The *Ark* emerged from hyperspace and immediately smashed into one of the battleships in the Coalition fleet, the ship once known as the *Athena*. The *Ark* had been filled with positron torpedoes and plutonium fusion warheads, and was a fleet crippling suicide bomb on its own. The impact destroyed both ships instantly, allowing only nanoseconds for the bot to engage the detonation device on the massive bomb. No known biological organism in the galaxy had reflexes fast enough to pull it off.

Dozens of vessels were wiped out in an instant by an explosion which shone brighter than the system's star. Cheers went up across the fleet channel. Miller sighed, relieved that phases one and two went more or less according to plan. All that remained was phase three.

30

Admiral Drex watched the massive, system wide, rings of the Vargon device spool up. He knew it would only be a few minutes before it was time for phase three of their attack. The Vargon bot stood with him in the CIC, alongside a skeleton crew. Every one of them knew it was a one way trip, and every one of them volunteered.

The chancellor had demanded that Drex remain with Admiral Yonk, aboard the *Vindicator*. He went on a rant about how Crom should command the *Kentucky* during phase three because they couldn't afford to lose Drex. They couldn't afford to lose a fleet admiral. But Drex would not have his first officer go down with the ship while he watched. And so, when the chancellor was safe at the rendezvous point, Drex sent Commander Crom over to the *Vindicator* in his place. Krell would have no choice but to understand. The man was not a military man, but Drex did know Krell to be a historian. And history was full of captains who went down with their ships.

Drex knew that if the Coalition was going to strike at their fleet then it would be another boarding party attacking through wormholes. He hoped that the chaos that the *Ark* had sewn would buy him the time to engage the super-weapon, but he wasn't so lucky.

It was Krynn who had come up with the plan. A plan so simple it was genius. All personnel across the fleet were outfitted with thick rubber soled boots and gloves. The troops who attacked the *Kentucky* before came in full exosuits, equipped with mag-boots. And it was the same when they came again, following the blow their fleet suffered when the *Ark* detonated.

When the first Coalition troops appeared, stepping through tears in reality and onto the Republic ships, they were accompanied by the same thick sulphuric smell. And Krynn's plan enacted automatically. Passively killing every single one of them moments after their arrival. The ships' life support computers were configured to detect any traces of sulphur in the atmosphere. When they did, power from electrical systems throughout the ship was conducted through the floors, frying the infiltrators in their power armor as the crew remained safe. Protected by their rubber boots. It was as simple a plan as it could be, and it worked with absolute efficiency.

Drex made sure that Krell gave Captain Krynn a medal for that idea. And he laughed to himself as the smell of charred flesh permeated the ship. Dozens of Coalition troops fried in an instant in and around the CIC. When it was over Drex ordered a sitrep from each of the other ships, and was relieved to hear that less than ten had been wounded, and only one killed across the fleet. Krynn's plan had been a massive success.

"Incoming fire, Admiral. The Coalition battleships' heavy batteries," a Master Chief whose name eluded Drex in the moment reported. "Shall we respond?"

"No, we'll be long gone before their fire is halfway here," the admiral said, dismissively. "Give the fleet the order to jump to the rendezvous point." Drex could not remember the name of the system where Krynn and Chancellor Krell awaited the fleet's arrival.

In seconds the fleet disappeared from the system, the *Kentucky* the only remaining Republican vessel. Admiral Drex turned to address his crew.

"What we do today, we do for the Republic, for mankind, for the galaxy! Each and every one of you has chosen to make the ultimate sacrifice, now, when no one else would step up. I could not be more proud than I am of you men and women, and it has been my honor to lead you into battle time and time again over these many years," Drex said, exuding the kind of energy that one of his station must in such a situation. Nothing but pure confidence. He'd already arranged with the Chancellor that each of the remaining crew of the *Kentucky* be posthumously awarded the Medal of Liberty. The Republic's highest award for military service. The medals would go to their families, but there was no higher honor in the Republic, military or civilian.

"Master Chief Ellis," Drex said, remembering the man's name. "On my mark."

The Admiral watched over the holoscreens as the Vargon device hummed in a gyroscopic blur. The ancient bot that stood beside him said, "Thank you, Admiral. You do for me what no other has been willing to provide."

"And what is that?" Drex asked. He was genuinely curious. "Death?"

"Yes, Admiral. Death," the bot said. "Now, it is time."

"Make the jump, Master Chief!"

The *Kentucky* tore through hyperspace, a very short distance in astronomical terms, and arrived within the core of the Talari star. Every bit of power the ship had was used to keep the shields operational. The moment shields went, the ship would be crushed by nearly immeasurable gravitational forces, smashed to nothing in an instant. The Vargon robot gave the admiral a nod, then flipped a switch on the little metal box it held, engaging the mantids' super-weapon.

Just as the Vargon star-eater began pulling the Talari star into their pocket dimension, the mantid device opened a wormhole to another star. The *Kentucky's* shields gave out, and it vaporized in a flash.

Where once a single star had been, there were two. And the star which came through the mantid wormhole was twenty times the mass of Talari, consuming the other star instantly. A moment later the new star sucked in upon itself, consuming all of its hydrogen fuel in a flash, then it was gone. Taken into the pocket dimension between real-space and hyperspace that the Vargon bot had called The Plane.

A moment later and the supernova would have destroyed dozens of systems, possibly hundreds. As it was, the ancient star-vampires got the biggest surprise in the three billion year history of their mighty race. Extinction.

What they had counted on being just another feast, another star to consume, was nothing other than their own undoing. The strange bubble between universes in which they made their existence popped in an instant. The explosion destroyed everything they ever built, everything they ever were, and everything they had ever known. A bomb with the power of five trillion suns took every bit of physical matter on The Plane and smashed it, trashed it, or vaporized it in an instant as the star's outer layers blew apart.

The remaining heart of the supernova collapsed into a black hole. The pocket dimension imploded in upon itself until it was nothing but a tear in reality.

EPILOGUE

Felo Krynn and his lyran copilot Lemmy had been drinking for hours. Krynn was so drunk that he couldn't recall the name of the cantina he was in, nor even of the world he was on. He wasn't even sure that if he walked out the front door that he'd find himself on a planet, or if he was on an asteroid. The past few weeks had been a blur.

Ever since the Battle of Talari the galaxy had been embroiled in a civil war. Or maybe wars was a better way to put it. The Confederation fought the Coalition for control of drak space. The Republic fought the Coalition for control of human space. And as of two days before, the Confederation and the Republic were at war. Krynn had lived through the first Great War, and he did not think that he would ever see another. Not since the galaxy had seen so many years of peace.

Krynn hadn't seen Miller since the fleet rendezvoused at Gorinthia after the battle. Not since the moment when she found out that it had been her father in command of the *Kentucky* at the end, and not Commander Crom. She'd been made a Lieutenant Commander, but she didn't seem to care. But Krynn got a subspace signal from her on a channel only used by Void Ops field agents. He didn't recall ever giving her the channel encryption, which made him smile. He always liked it when his life validated his assumptions, and Miller making a good spy was one such assumption he had made.

She gave him coordinates to meet at…wherever it was that they found themselves. The name of which Krynn still could not recall. He wondered why she wouldn't risk telling him over subspace comms. He was sure that the situation was serious if this was her preferred method of contact. Krynn had heard through the grapevine that Fleet Admiral Yonk had given her command of her own battlecruiser and that she declined the post to serve the OCR directly.

Another hour went by, and Krynn ate some flat fried bread that was on the bar's menu. Though it was far too hard for his taste it did him good to have something on his stomach other than daigor vodka. He was getting annoyed, and a little worried when Lemmy snorted and gave him a nudge with his hairy elbow.

"Miller's here?" he asked, as he straightened his jacket and dusted breadcrumbs off his collar.

Lemmy looked over Krynn's shoulder and nodded. Felo turned on his barstool to see Miller setting next to him at the bar. She wore a light exosuit, and had a one-off custom helmet sitting on the bar. Krynn was used to seeing her in her dress uniform or her Spartan exosuit power armor, not in the sleek grey and black of Void Ops hunter-killers.

"Good to see you, Miller," he said. "I didn't even hear you come in."

"Krell's been kidnapped," she said, wasting no time. The bartender poured her a drink. "The Coalition has him."

"And how did that...I mean...what? Kidnapped?" Krynn stammered. "Ever since the Battle of Talari the chancellor has been surrounded by his praetorians. Or at least that is what I thought was the case...that's what I heard."

"It was Slaath," Miller said before throwing back her glass as if it were a single shot and signaling the bartender for another. "He's Coalition. He opened fire on a council meeting aboard *Space Force One*, killing several before grabbing Krell and engaging one of those damn wormhole generators."

"And nobody noticed he was carrying around one of those boxes?" Krynn asked, stunned.

"It must have been built into his cybernetics. As well as the weapon he used. However he did it, he took great care to avoid detection," Miller said. She set her glass down and turned to face Krynn. "Felo. I have other bad news."

Krynn didn't say anything, just nodded to let her know he was as ready for whatever it was that she had to say as he'd ever be.

"He killed the first lady," Miller said. "Shot her through the eye."

"Well, that's not such bad news. I mean, they back those androids up regularly. She's probably already in a brand new body, advocating for some idealistic cause or another," Krynn said.

"Slaath killed many people in the attack, Krynn," Miller said. She was angry and wrestling with herself, trying to say what she had to say.

"Jeru, Miller, just tell me already," Krynn said.

"He shot Royce. Right through the heart. I held her as she died in my arms," Miller finally said. "Her last words were…"

It was nearly a minute before she could find the strength to continue. Krynn could tell that Miller was not using mood enhancers. He was shaken to the core, but in the moment felt great empathy for her. He was a drunken mess, but she was an emotional wreck.

"She wanted me to tell you that she loved you, and that she wished that she never frakked things up between you," Miller said. She ordered another drink by tapping her glass, downed it, and swallowed down her feelings. Miller stood up from her barstool and turned toward the door.

"Well, aren't you coming?" she asked Krynn, as if she had never mentioned Royce.

"Where, to save the galaxy again? I've had enough of that, Syn," Felo Krynn said. He didn't admit it, but he was concerned about her emotional state.

"No, Krynn. This time it isn't about saving the galaxy. It isn't about stopping a war. No, the war has already started. It isn't about the Republic, or humanity, or any of those things."

"Then tell me what what it *is* about, Miller."

"Revenge," she said as she walked toward the exit. Syn Miller did not turn to see them, but she knew Krynn and Lemmy followed close behind.

THANKS FOR READING!

You can keep up with the author through his website www.aleisterdavidson.com or at any of the social media sites below.

And if you have the time, please consider leaving a review at the point of purchase (most likely Amazon).
This helps other readers to discover the book, and I am very grateful to all readers who leave reviews.

facebook.com/AleisterDavidson

instagram.com/aleisterdavidson

bookbub.com/profile/aleister-davidson

pinterest.com/EastBayHorror

www.ingramcontent.com/pod-product-compliance
Lightning Source LLC
Chambersburg PA
CBHW030243200626
46816CB00002BA/493